RETURN TO

Hawk's Hill

ALSO BY ALLAN W. ECKERT

RETURN TO

Hawk's Hill

A NOVEL

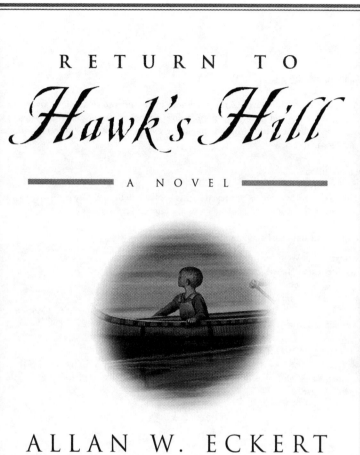

ALLAN W. ECKERT

Little, Brown and Company
Boston   New York   Toronto   London

Copyright © 1998 by Allan W. Eckert

First Edition

The characters and events portrayed in this book are fictitious. Any similarity to real persons, living or dead, is coincidental and not intended by the author.

Library of Congress Cataloging-in-Publication Data

Eckert, Allan W.
    Return to Hawk's Hill : a novel / Allan W. Eckert. — 1st ed.
        p.   cm.
    Sequel to: Incident at Hawk's Hill.
    Summary: Running away from a vicious trapper, seven-year-old Ben MacDonald is separated from his family and eventually ends up on the shores of Lake Winnipeg, where he is taken in by a tribe of Metis Indians.
    ISBN 0-316-21593-7
    [1. Survival — Fiction.   2. Metis Indians — Fiction.   3. Indians of North America — Northwest, Canadian — Fiction.   4. Canada — Fiction.   I. Title.
    PZ7.E1978Re   1998
    [Fic] — dc21   97-40786

10 9 8 7 6 5 4 3 2

MV-NY

Published simultaneously in Canada
by Little, Brown & Company (Canada) Limited

Printed in the United States of America

To all those thousands of youngsters

— in heart as well as in age —

who have written to me over the past

quarter of a century in their enthusiasm for

Incident at Hawk's Hill

and who fervently hoped for a sequel,

this book is sincerely and gratefully dedicated

ACKNOWLEDGMENT

The author would like to express sincere thanks to Father Gerard Beaudet of North Battleford, Saskatchewan, for his expert help with the Cree Indian words and phrases used in this book. Father Beaudet, who has spent his life as a priest among the Crees of Manitoba and Saskatchewan, is the author of the *Cree-English, English-Cree Dictionary* (Wuerz Publishing Ltd., Winnipeg, Manitoba), the only published work of its kind.

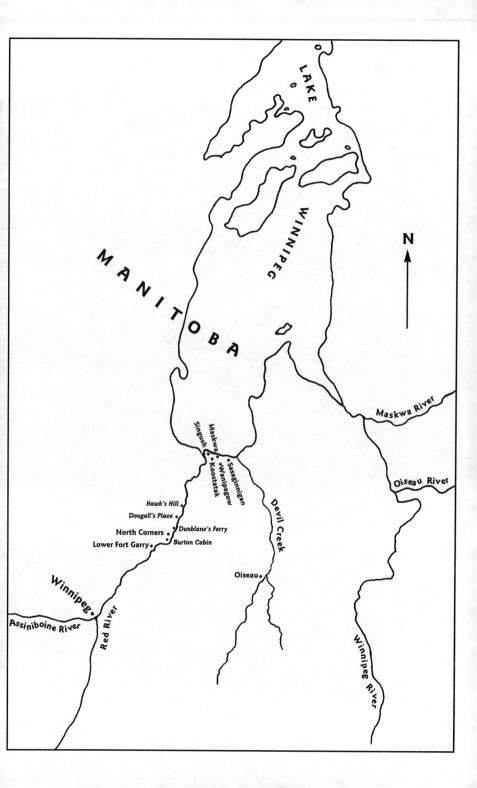

RETURN TO
Hawk's Hill

PROLOGUE

The big female badger had died at dawn. Throughout the night, the MacDonald family had nursed her, their focal point the flicker of life that continued to glint in her barely open eyes. They wished they could help her more, but there was nothing else they could do. William MacDonald had been careful not to raise the hopes of Esther and the children with false optimism. Esther had checked the terrible wound a few times as her four children looked on soberly, and she had swabbed it once with a warm damp cloth, but it was to no avail. Both Beth and Coral had cried quietly, once together and once separately, and occasionally dozed in their chairs. John, eldest of the four youngsters, features frozen in a non-expression, simply sat and waited.

And then there was Ben.

Youngest of the family, he was uncommonly small for a six-year-old. That characteristic was what had enabled him to take refuge from a storm by squeezing into a badger hole when he'd become lost in the prairie to the west of Hawk's Hill. The female badger, who had just lost her entire litter of pups, had bristled when she caught his scent and had entered her den cautiously but sensed at once that he posed no threat to her. The initial fear between them quickly disappeared, and they formed a bond. It was a bond born of loneliness and loss, a bond that grew and strengthened in their mutual fear of the big trapper, George Burton. As one of the many searchers who had volunteered to look for the missing Ben, Burton was the first person Ben saw when he started to emerge from the den. Unseen by the trapper, the boy had instinctively ducked back into the den and had remained there to avoid being discovered by this man who had so frightened him not long before, when he had visited at Hawk's Hill with his big yellow dog, Lobo. This man, Ben could tell, was every bit as vicious as his dog, the kind of man who was capable of brutally destroying wildlife with no sense of mercy or remorse.

The big female badger also had good reason to fear Burton. The trapper had caught and killed her mate, and then she, too, had been caught by two toes in a steel trap he had set near her den. For days she had listened helplessly to the cries of her offspring in the den, cries of hunger that grew ever weaker and finally ceased. And when at last she gnawed off her own two imprisoned toes and entered the den, she had found that all the pups in her litter were dead.

The maternal instinct still at a high level in the badger, she had brought Ben food—eggs, frogs, mice, and snakes—and Ben had treated her wounded paw in the only way he could, by licking it until the swelling and fever were gone and the healing process well begun. This unlikely pair had found fulfillment in each other of very basic needs, and for eight weeks they had shared their lives. During that interval, they had even slain the trapper's big dog, which had been bent on killing the badger—and the boy as well, if it came to that.

Then Ben had at last been found by his brother and taken home to Hawk's Hill, the female badger following. As the badger had more or less adopted Ben, the MacDonald family more or less adopted the badger. Ben was finally beginning to emerge from the shell of extreme shyness that had for so long enveloped him.

With summer at an end, he would soon be enrolled in school for the first time, and he was looking forward to it.

All had seemed well until yesterday, when George Burton had ridden in and, seeing the badger by the house, instantly shot her, the powerful bullet striking her on one side and passing out the other. A confrontation between the MacDonalds and Burton had followed, in which the heavily bearded trapper first threatened Ben's father with his rifle, then wounded him and, when attacked by John, knocked the sixteen-year-old youth unconscious. He desisted only when Ben's mother leveled a rifle at his chest and threatened to shoot him. And so William MacDonald had ordered Burton away, never again to show his face at Hawk's Hill, on risk of being killed. It had been a traumatic experience for all.

The greatest trauma was experienced by Ben. They all had thought the badger was dead, and Ben, refusing to let anyone help, set out to bury her, carrying the big limp body with difficulty. But then her eyes had opened with life, and he had hurriedly brought her back, to be nursed throughout this long night just ended. But the badger was too severely injured.

Now, bumping across the rolling Manitoba prairie that was taking on its late summer hue of light tan, the

MacDonald family had come in their wagon to the rocky little outcrop projecting from the earth about a mile west of Hawk's Hill. The bullet wound in the elder MacDonald's side, which had been well treated by Esther, was a mere graze and in no way serious, but it was painful, causing him to wince when the wagon hit hard bumps, and he was relieved when the short trip was finished. As if by mutual agreement, before alighting, they all looked at the low outcropping of rocks close by. Beneath that pile was the den Ben had shared with the big female badger and where she would now remain forever.

With a fragile new rapport established between them, the elder MacDonald was wise enough to let Ben decide how matters should be handled here. As Esther and the two girls got out and stood soberly to one side, William and John, at Ben's request, lifted the dead badger from the wagon bed and lay her close to the den's entrance—a roughly circular hole in the earth some twenty inches in diameter—and then they, too, stood back. The hole in the prairie grass was more than ten feet from the rocks.

Ben squatted close to the badger for a while, silently looking at her, then finally reached out and placed his hand on her head. After a moment he turned and looked at the hole. It was important to him that she be placed in the den, not merely in the passageway leading to it. He knew he could not push the body ahead of him down to the den, so he thrust his legs into the opening first and began inching his way backward and downward. Until now the MacDonalds had all assumed that the badger would simply be placed well down the hole and then covered over, but now the realization of what Ben planned struck them. Beth and Coral audibly sucked in their breath, and Esther, concerned, started stepping forward, preparing to say something, but she stopped without speaking when her husband grasped her arm and faintly shook his head. Only John appeared unsurprised by what his little brother was doing.

When Ben was in the hole up to midchest, he reached out and grasped the badger's forelegs and pulled her to him. There was little room to spare on any side of the hole, even though he had enlarged it considerably while he was there with the badger, but he gradually disappeared and the dead animal was slowly pulled out of sight after him. It was many long minutes before Ben, struggling doggedly with his burden, finally reached the principal den. The burrow angled downward for five feet before leveling off and moving another ten feet until directly beneath the rock pile. Here the actual den chamber was about four feet in diameter and three feet high, the top domed so steeply among the rocks above that it was nearly conical. Vague filtered light came through cracks between the rocks, making barely visible the matted prairie grasses and mosses that covered the floor.

It was when Ben got the badger's body inside the den that the memory of the days and weeks he had spent here with her crashed down upon him with unbearable weight and he began to sob uncontrollably. After a little while, when the crying subsided, he reached out and picked up her right paw, and touched his fingers to the place where she had lost the two toes. He let his hand move gently up her leg to her head and caressed her ears, faintly smiling through his tears as he felt the distinctive deep notch in the left one — the mark of an old injury. And then he cried hard again.

At last he looked at her one final time, whispered, "Oh, badger," and turned away. Without looking back or paying any attention to the smaller emergency escape tunnel also connecting to the den, he slid headfirst into the main tunnel and squirmed with relative ease and quickness to the surface. So long had he been out of sight that his family had become concerned for his safety, fearing there had been a cave-in. Now they moved close and embraced him and then, at his direction, carried a number of smaller rocks from the pile and stuffed them down not only the main hole but into the entry of the emergency escape burrow as well, some fifty feet from the rock pile. That done, William and John shoveled dirt over the top until all trace of the burrows was obliterated.

And then the MacDonald family, silent but close in heart, returned to Hawk's Hill.

CHAPTER  1

When the children streamed out of the front double doors of the big white clapboard schoolhouse in North Corners, they yelled and jumped and shrieked more than usual, because this had been the last day of the school year. It was now mid-May, with a full summer lying ahead of them, and they were bubbling with excitement as they imagined all the wonderful things they might experience before school resumed in September.

The three younger MacDonald children chattered about many things on the way home, but most of all about how well little Ben, just turned seven, had done in his first year at school. His teacher and schoolmates had all expected that, at best, he would be slower in grasping things. After all, everyone knew how withdrawn he was, even with his own family, and that he rarely spoke to anyone except his mother.

But even more, this was the little boy who had gained notoriety, from Winnipeg northward, as "the wild child," a youngster who not only preferred the company of animals—especially wild animals—to the company of people but who was able to mimic the actions and sounds of birds or mammals with such accuracy that many thought he was actually able to converse with them. That, of course, was not true, but it made a good story, and the fact was, most animals, whether wild or domestic, were so unafraid of him that they allowed him to approach very closely. In many cases, he had even been able to reach out and touch them.

Then there was the badger incident of a year ago, which everyone in the region and beyond had heard about. Most people had also heard how the trapper George Burton had killed the badger, and they had concluded that this would surely make the boy even more withdrawn.

However, not only had little Ben MacDonald become much more open and vocal with his own family, but he even talked freely with other children and only became excessively shy when meeting unfamiliar adults. The greatest surprise was his performance in school. He did far more than eke by in his lessons; he excelled, showing himself to be more astute than his classmates and even quicker in learning than many of the students a grade or two advanced of his. His excellent schoolwork and the fact that his detailed knowledge of nature astounded the teachers had added considerably to the sense of wonder with which he was viewed by others. It was a credit to the boy that instead of letting this go to his head and becoming prideful, he was able to maintain an innocent charm. Just about everyone, it seemed, really liked Ben MacDonald.

As soon as school had been dismissed today, the three younger children had raced to the nearby road where their seventeen-year-old brother, John, sat patiently awaiting them in the two-seater buggy. His school — North Corners High School — was on the other side of town, and this had also been his last day of classes. Beth, four years younger, climbed into the front seat with him while Coral, now ten, and Ben scrambled into the rear. It was a ten-mile drive to Hawk's Hill, and the children chattered and giggled during the ride, with Beth, as usual, tending to dominate Coral and Ben. All three adored their older brother, a competent and self-assured young man who handled horse and carriage skillfully as they followed the familiar rutted wagon road paralleling the northward-flowing Red River.

The farther north they rode, the fewer houses and farms they saw, and as the road became less traveled, it diminished until it was hardly more than a pair of wagon tracks. Now, a bit over an hour after leaving North Corners, they emerged from the trees flanking the river and entered the rolling prairie land, angling slightly away from the river. The way was smoother here, with no more hard emergent roots to bump over. They were only about a mile and a half south of Hawk's Hill, with one last intervening knoll between them and home. Just after they passed the southern foot of that knoll and were nearing halfway to its low crest, Ben, who had been silent for a while, suddenly spoke.

"John," he said, "could you stop here, please?"

"Why?" John swiveled on his seat to look at his little brother.

"Prob'ly 'cause he has to do his business," Coral piped up, snickering.

"Coral!" It was Beth. "That's terrible. You ought to be ashamed of yourself. I'm going to tell Mama what you said."

"Go ahead, smarty-pants, I don't —"

"Okay, you two," John broke in, "that's enough." He looked at Ben and again said, "Why?"

Ben hunched his shoulders a little and said, "I'd just sort of like to walk the rest of the way through the fields. Maybe see a prairie chicken with a nestful of eggs or something. You know."

"Guess it wouldn't hurt." John reined the horse to a stop and as Ben alighted from the right side of the rig, added, "Straight home, now, hear? No wandering off."

"And," put in Coral, still trying to be funny, "don't step in any badger holes!" She giggled, but then, when a pained expression appeared on Ben's face and he lowered his eyes and shook his head faintly, she was immediately contrite. "Oh, I'm sorry, Ben. I just said that without thinking. I didn't mean . . ." Her voice trailed off.

"I'm going to tell Mama what you said," Beth snapped, reiterating that tiresome expression of hers.

Coral flared back, "Don't be so bossy!"

"It's okay, Coral," Ben murmured. He raised his head, brightening a bit. "You and Beth want to come along?"

"No," they replied in unison.

"Like I said, Ben," John told him in a no-fooling tone, "straight home."

"I will. I promise."

John nodded, then snapped the reins and clucked, and the horse lurched forward. Tossing a little wave at the girls, who waved back, Ben watched them head away for a moment and then set off through the grasses to the right of the road. Actually, even though he would have enjoyed their company, he was glad his sisters had declined, knowing he was apt to observe much more prairie life by silently moving alone than with those two, who were always giggling, talking, or arguing.

The new grasses were already more than knee high, with small clumps of bushes growing here and there. He walked a dozen or so paces away from the road and then turned left to follow a parallel course to it toward the farm, with the broad, tree-fringed Red River a hundred yards distant to his right. His keen gaze glimpsed a grassy formation that was a little different. He knelt and carefully parted the stems and was delighted when he saw a nest with — he counted quickly — eleven eggs. About an inch and a quarter long each, the eggs were a buff color, and a few had scattered speckles of darker brown. He reached forward and gently touched one, grinning at the warmth. The prairie hen had evidently slipped away noiselessly at his approach and was probably still close by, but he decided not to disturb her or the nest any more than he already had.

He carefully pushed the grasses back up into place, then stood and glanced after the carriage again, which was just now topping the knoll about a hundred yards away and starting down the other side. He watched it disappear as he began walking again, stepping carefully away from the nest, but before he had walked a dozen paces farther, he heard a distant sharp yell from John, immediately followed by the screaming of his sisters. Instantly he raced toward the crest, dodging bushes, the grasses swishing across his legs. As he topped the hill, he slammed to a halt, momentarily frozen.

Well ahead on the road, John was furiously galloping the rig toward home, which was visible in the distance, and the girls were hanging on grimly. Much closer to Ben, sideways to him and motionless in the road, was a horseman who was staring after the carriage. Even though the man was not directly facing him, Ben recognized the barrel-chested bulk and heavy black beard of George Burton.

Terrified, the boy dropped flat to the ground, crawled to a nearby bush, and then came to his knees to peer through it. Burton, right hand holding the reins and left hand resting on one of the two big saddlebags, was still watching the buggy, but then he turned and kneed his mount forward on the road in Ben's direction. Squirming even deeper into cover, the boy watched as the trapper came closer, the huge man's head swiveling back and forth as he scanned the fields on both sides of the road. He seemed to be looking for something, and the conviction rose in Ben that he was himself the object of the scrutiny. It seemed more than merely plausible to the boy that Burton, seeing the other three children fleeing, surmised that Ben was somewhere close by and was searching for him in order to take an easy revenge against the Mac-Donald family.

Now no more than fifty feet distant, Burton, clad in the same greasy leathers he always wore, trotted his horse without pause past Ben's hiding place. Halfway down the south side of the knoll, however, he stopped and stood high in the stirrups, shading his eyes with one hand and again studying the surrounding terrain closely. Thankful that John, Beth, and Coral had gotten away, Ben dropped to his stomach again, and his fears were confirmed when he heard Burton call aloud.

"Yo, boy! You hidin'?" The voice paused for a moment and then went on. "You better, 'cause if I catch you, you're gonna pay fer all the trouble you an' your damn fam'ly have caused me. You hear?"

Ben's heart was thudding with the fear that Burton would see the trail he had made through the grasses. The man was skilled in tracking, and Ben knew that if Burton saw the trail, he would follow it and eventually find him, and he didn't dare just lie there and wait to be discovered.

Without risking putting his head up to see where the big man was now, Ben began squirming through the grasses toward the river. It seemed to him that it took forever to get there, but at last he was among the larger trees and brush, with the big, swiftly flowing Red River only a few yards ahead of him. Seeing the water triggered a thought: his father's rowboat! It was moored to the shore, as was customary, and couldn't be very far to the north from here. If he could get to it, he could untie the rope, jump in, and float downstream until he was well away from here. Then he could row back to shore and make it to the house in a roundabout way without being seen.

Still not daring to risk trying to see where Burton was now, lest he be seen himself, Ben came to his feet and began running through the riverine growth as fast as he could, following the shore downstream while simultaneously dodging trees and brush. He was actually farther than he had thought from where the boat was moored, perhaps two hundred yards or more, but he continued running and dodging until, finally, there it was. The clunky old wooden rowboat, floating in a little cove in the shoreline, was tied by a length of medium-heavy rope to the trunk of a small cottonwood tree.

He tore frantically at the knot, which in his father's strong hands would have loosened at once. In his smaller and weaker grasp, however, it was loosening much too slowly. At one point in his efforts he paused and cocked his head, thinking he'd heard something. He had, and the sound came only too clearly now—the drumming of galloping hooves. Burton! His terror rose again, and he tore at the knot with renewed frenzy and then gasped aloud with relief when at last it slid apart and fell free from the tree. He pulled the boat in until the bow touched shore, then leaped aboard, almost losing a shoe in the mud in the process. His movement thrust the cumbersome craft outward, beyond the little eddy that swirled in the cove; it skimmed into the swifter water, turned in a half circle, and then steadied, floating broadside to the current. Ben dropped to the planked flooring and lay there beneath the level of the gunwales, heart hammering, for fully three minutes as the boat drifted with increasing speed.

At last he dared to raise his head and look cautiously about. No one was in sight. All he could see was the swift, gurgling water and the dense growth of trees silently flanking both shores. A raccoon snuffling about on the near shore raised itself erect to watch more closely, then dropped to all fours and disappeared into the brush.

For the first time since the instant he had glimpsed Burton, Ben relaxed a little, blowing out a large puff of air in relief. A quartet of crows launched themselves from a tree on the near shore, then flew in a floppy pattern across the broad river and disappeared over the distant trees rimming the far shore, some fifty yards or more to the east. Ben looked at the water and, considering how fast the current was pushing the boat along, estimated that surely by now he was safe from the trapper and could row to shore and run home unseen. He reached down for the oars that were always stored in the bottom of the boat and then stopped, eyes widening. They weren't there!

And now a new kind of fear filled little Ben MacDonald.

CHAPTER 2

Back at the road near the crest of the hill, the hoofbeats Ben had heard and that had terrified him so were actually not those of the trapper George Burton's mount. They were instead those of his father's and brother's horses.

Shortly before, immediately upon thundering up Hawk's Hill and pounding to a stop at the house, John was yelling even as he leaped from the buggy and while the horse was still nervously dancing in its traces. Hearing the commotion, Esther and William rushed out of the house onto the porch and listened with rising fear as John blurted out what had happened, while the sobbing Coral and Beth climbed out of the buggy and added their disjointed accounts. The girls ran to their mother and clung to her while William and John dashed to the barn and swiftly saddled their horses.

By the time they finished and rode to the house, Esther had calmed the carriage horse and tied the reins to the hitching rail in front. She had then left the girls standing wide-eyed on the porch and raced inside, returning a moment later with her husband's and son's rifles and a handful of extra shells. These she handed to William as she murmured, "Be careful," her voice much more calm than she was feeling.

William had nodded grimly and touched her hand briefly as he took the guns and cartridges. He handed the smaller gun and some of the shells to John, and both father and son quickly opened the chambers of their weapons and loaded them. Then William kneed his horse into a gallop, stuffing the extra loose shells into his pocket as he did so. John pocketed his few extra cartridges and, with a little wave to his mother and sisters, followed closely behind.

A few minutes later, having thundered up the wagon trail to the crest of the smaller knoll, they pulled their horses to a stop and studied the surroundings carefully. There was no sign of Burton or his horse, but neither was Ben anywhere to be seen. John led his father to the spot where Ben had gotten out of the buggy, but they could see no traces of him, although occasionally the fresh hoof marks of Burton's horse were evident along the wagon road.

When they stood high in their stirrups and shouted Ben's name time and again, there was no response. The only sound that reached their ears was the high-pitched *kreeeeee* of a circling hawk and the rustling of the grasses as breezes touched down, the tips of the foliage bowing beneath them in long swatches, as if an invisible squadron of boats were passing. Remembering only too well how his little son had once before been frightened by the big trapper, William shook his head.

"He may be hiding. Scared. Did you see which way he started off?"

"I didn't look back," John admitted. "I don't know." His voice was husky with contained emotion, and he swept an arm out in a motion that took in the wide expanse of prairie west of the road. "Probably out that way."

William grunted in agreement. "Let's spread out and range."

They did so, staying in sight of each other and wheeling this way and that through the thick new growth, occasionally calling Ben's name and listening for a response that never came. Prairie chickens burst from cover with noisy, rapid wing beats, flew short distances, and then disappeared as they landed in the dense grasses. A hunting red fox, pausing in midstride with one forefoot lifted, stared at them for an instant, then ducked and vanished.

For close to an hour the pair searched before finally coming together again near where they had begun, and then the elder MacDonald voiced the fearful thought that had been rising in them both.

"Looks like Burton may have gotten him. We've spent too much time here. Let's go. We'll follow the road and try to overtake them."

The trail the trapper's horse had left, heading toward North Corners, was easy enough to follow and became all the more apparent as the wagon road broadened and became less grass-covered. The sun was just setting when the two riders reached the first in a cluster of houses. It was Edgar Dougall's place, and he was out working in his garden patch. Dougall was one of those many area residents who had helped in the futile search for Ben when the boy had disappeared almost a year ago. Now the man paused as they approached and leaned on his hoe, a small frown furrowing his brow.

"William, John," he said in greeting. "Why the guns? Trouble?"

William responded with a question of his own. "Did you see George Burton pass here a little while ago?"

Dougall took off his hat and wiped his forehead with the back of his wrist. "Well, I dunno for sure. Maybe."

"What's that mean?" John blurted out, more sharply than intended.

"Means I seen a rider, boy." A testiness had come into Edgar's voice at John's tone. "Might've been Burton. Might not've been. That's what it means."

"Ed," William spoke again, "we don't mean to be short, but this is important. You know Burton well enough to recognize him, so how come you're not sure?"

" 'Cause he was already past me when I looked up. All's I seen was his back. Ain't seen 'im in over a year, but it looked like Burton from the rear. Looked like his horse, too. Big packs on the horse, like Burton usually has. Rode right on through without stopping. Heading for Winnipeg, I guess. What the devil's going on, William?"

"Ben's missing. Burton was out by our place and scared the kids. Now Ben's gone. We think Burton took him. Followed his tracks to here. Did the rider have a little boy in the saddle with him?"

Dougall shook his head. "Didn't see one. Prob'ly wouldn't've, though, if he had the boy in the saddle in front of him, big as he is and small as your boy is. And what with those big saddlebags and all."

The nebulosity of the response irked MacDonald, but he curbed his irritation. "How long ago was it he rode through, Ed?"

"Not too long. Half hour, maybe. Maybe even an hour. You really think Burton would've taken Ben?"

There was no response, as the MacDonalds had already wheeled their horses and put them into a gallop. Dougall stared after them and then shook his head. "That Ben," he muttered, turning back to his hoeing. "He sure can get folks stirred up."

Having scattered several clusters of chickens pecking in the dirt road as they raced through the little community, William and John picked up Burton's track again as it headed south, and they pushed their mounts even harder. Twilight was upon them now, and the tracks were harder to see, but it seemed evident where the trapper was heading. With luck, they might be able to overtake him before he could reach ten-mile-distant Winnipeg.

As a matter of fact, the rider Edgar Dougall had seen from the rear was indeed George Burton, but he was not on his way to Winnipeg at all. Unaware that he was the object of pursuit, only a little over two miles south of North Corners he had left the Winnipeg road and angled southeastwardly toward the little ramshackle cabin he had built long ago on the west bank of the Red River near a fording place, when he was trapping in this area. He had several cabins like this throughout the region, for his traplines often stretched twenty miles or more as they followed various streams, large and small.

With the exception of Dunblane's Ferry, just a little northeast of North Corners and located about five miles downstream from here, this fording place was the only relatively easy crossing in the more than fifty-mile stretch between Winnipeg and where this broad, powerful river emptied into Lake Winnipeg. It was a crossing used mainly by the Indians living in the territory east of here, between the Red River and the Winnipeg River, and by the soldiers stationed at Lower Fort Garry, some two miles or so west of the cabin, on the road to Winnipeg.

Burton had been traveling all day, and he was tired. It was his intention to prepare himself something to eat and get a good night's sleep in the old cabin. In the morning he would ride his horse across the ford and head for the upper reaches of Devil Creek, the location of the Cree village he called Wa-zo but which was spelled Oiseau. It was named after its old chief, Oiseleur — Bird-Catcher — with whom Burton had traded for many years, getting fine fur pelts in exchange for the goods they needed, which all too often included such forbidden trade items as guns, ammunition, and liquor.

Planning to spend upward of a week talking trade with Oiseleur and his people to determine what they most needed or wanted, Burton decided that when he had finished business at Oiseau, he would then return to the Red River and follow its east bank downstream—northward—some forty miles to its mouth. Lake Winnipeg, third largest lake in Canada, was a huge body of water onto which he had rarely ventured because it could become treacherous if bad weather developed. Other traders with whom he was familiar, and who plied the waters much more frequently than he, had told him it was as much as seventy miles wide in places and stretched more than 260 miles to the north, where its outlet waters became the great Nelson River, which eventually flowed into Hudson Bay. He had even heard stories that hundreds of years earlier, the Norsemen, having crossed the Atlantic, entered Hudson Bay, ascended the Nelson River to Lake Winnipeg, and may have even tried to ascend the Red River.

All that, however, was of little interest to Burton. What concerned him more was the fact that near the point where the Red River flowed into Lake Winnipeg were numerous villages of the Metis—a subculture of the Crees, made up primarily of people of mixed French and Cree ancestry.[*] Because he so often took advantage of the Indians wherever he traded, he had

---

*The word *Metis* is both singular and plural. In the singular it is pronounced MAY-tee, in the plural MAY-teez.

few friends among the Metis, but since he was the only trader who stopped by on a relatively regular basis, they tolerated him and had little choice but to accept the outrageous prices he charged them for the goods he brought. And now, with the strife continuing between the Metis and the Canadian government, these Indians were going to need more guns and ammunition.

Burton licked his lips in anticipation at the thought.

THE ROAD TO WINNIPEG led directly past Lower Fort Garry, and William and John MacDonald paused here in the deepening dusk to ask the same questions they had put to Dougall. The commanding officer, Captain James Stuart, after listening to William's queries, summoned the two guards on sentry duty and was assured by both that no one had passed on the road for more than two hours.

Obviously then, this meant that in the gathering twilight, William and John had missed seeing where Burton turned off or in which direction he had headed. They thanked Captain Stuart and grimly prepared to ride on the remaining few miles into Winnipeg to inform officials. Fortunately, it was not necessary; the commander told them that when they arrived, he had just been preparing to send a dispatch to their parent Fort Garry in Winnipeg, and so he would have the messenger stop by the constabulary and make an official report. Declining the officer's kind invitation that they have something to eat before setting out again, they thanked him and left.

Now, wearily and dejectedly riding back toward Hawk's Hill and prepared to resume their search for Ben in the morning near where he had alighted from the wagon, the father and son fell silent. Neither was willing to put into words the strong conviction that had arisen in both—that what they would ultimately find then would be Ben's body.

CHAPTER 3

The initial surge of raw terror that had flooded Ben MacDonald when he realized he was adrift on the Red River with no oars quickly dwindled. It did not, however, disappear because he was only too aware of the peril of his predicament.

The only thing in the bottom of the boat was a large old cloth fish bag, so at first he tried to paddle with his hands, lying on the bow and pulling at the water with both hands. But the wooden rowboat was much too cumbersome for him to have much effect against such a current, and he was soon exhausted from the effort. He slumped back and watched the silent parade of flanking trees slide past, trying to envision what might lie ahead.

Far upstream, his father had told him, the Red River and the Assiniboine River, which converged at Winnipeg, were both known to be treacherous, with numerous violent rapids. Downstream from Winnipeg, however, while certainly deserving of considerable caution, the Red River, now with the waters of the Assiniboine merged into it, was much broader but not quite so hazardous. The current was very powerful, of course, but the remaining cascades before reaching the lake were relatively few and comparatively small. Nevertheless, they could be deadly, his father had warned, and most probably *would* be to a small boy alone in a boat—which was why it had been forbidden for him to venture out on the river by himself. It was a restriction he had always observed, until now. He was sure that had the oars been in the boat, he would have been able to maneuver it to shore. Without the oars, however . . .

Suddenly Ben MacDonald was crying.

After a long while his sobbing faded away, and once again there was no sound but the ever-present gurgling of the water as the current swept him along. On a few occasions, where the river bent in sinuous curves, the boat drifted fairly close to shore, but never quite close enough for Ben to thrust the boat in even closer. Not a good swimmer to begin with, Ben was smart enough to realize that it would be foolhardy in the extreme to risk his life by jumping into the water and trying to make it to shore.

While the river was his paramount concern, another bothersome thought kept rising. Indians. Ben knew there were several Metis villages near the river's mouth, and he knew as well, especially from discussions between his parents at the dinner table, that a wave of friction between the Metis and the Canadian government had begun three years ago and that some skirmishes had even occurred. It was being called the Red River Rebellion. The causes were clear enough: The Metis were upset that the government had been usurping their hereditary lands in this great river valley and had then been giving or selling it to farmers and settlers.

For a while the Half-Breeds, as William MacDonald and most of the area's white residents called the Metis, had even taken over control of Fort Garry in Winnipeg and set up a provisional government. They had remained there until the Canadians had met some of their demands. Since then, there had been several disturbing confrontations between the Metis and Canadian soldiers on patrols, and as a result, the farmers and settlers remained on edge. There was good reason,

William declared: The conflict was reportedly broadening to include incidents between the Metis and white civilians. The Indians were complaining of escalating mistreatment at the hands of the white settlers, and the whites complained of fences having been torn down, stock released, and lone travelers being insulted or even roughed up by Metis and being told they must leave this country or suffer the consequences.

Even among the children at school wild stories were circulating. Especially fanciful and frightening accounts stemmed from older boys attempting to impress or scare the younger students: stories of the Metis kidnapping white children who were never heard from again, scary stories told in whispers that the missing children had been tortured and then cut into little pieces and fed to dogs. None of the wide-eyed younger children—and few of the older ones—thought to question the fact that no one knew personally of anyone who had ever disappeared in such a manner.

Ben's own father had little patience with these Indians and spoke of them often with disdain and occasionally with flagrant contempt, always referring to them as Half-Breeds and troublemakers. With the MacDonald farm at Hawk's Hill the closest to the Metis villages, even though they were on the opposite side of the big river, William MacDonald was vocal in his belief that an attack against the farm was imminent. He wished that the Indians would just go away and leave the farmers and settlers in peace. After all, he contended, it was the whites who were undergoing privation and hardship to make this land productive, while the Metis, as he put it, "just want to let it lie fallow and use it all as their own private hunting ground."

During one such dinner-table tirade, Esther suggested that he was being unfair. The land had been occupied by the Indians first, she pointed out, and they undoubtedly felt, with justification, that they had a right to use it in any way they cared to. William responded angrily, and a heated exchange erupted between them. It was the only time Ben had ever heard his parents quarrel, and it had made him sad and confused, even though the two made up soon afterward. Not knowing who was right or wrong and unwilling to take sides, he wound up holding the Indians to blame, even though deep down it made him uncomfortable to do so.

Hours had now passed since he had started floating downstream in the rowboat, and it was turning cooler in the gathering gloom of twilight. He was already shivering, and he knew that the temperature would drop even more during the night. He picked up the big dirty fish bag, which had originally been a feed sack.

He wrinkled his nose at its fishy smell but overcame his distaste and thrust his feet into it. When he pulled it up as far as he could, it reached almost to his armpits. By bending his legs and scrunching down inside, he was able to put his arms inside and bring it over his shoulders, then clench it together at his neck.

For whatever meager protection it might provide, he scooched and squirmed until, with some difficulty, he managed to get under the broad plank that made up the center seat of the rowboat. There he huddled, shivering, in the bottom of the boat against the darkening chill of nightfall, wondering if he would survive the rapids; wondering, if he did, if he would be caught by the Metis; wondering, if that occurred, if they would torture him and cut him up; wondering, in fact, if this were to be the last night of his life. It was in this state of mind, hungry and cold and beset with an exhaustion that was both physical and mental, that he finally fell into a fitful sleep.

He partially awakened numerous times during the long night, always scrunching himself into a tighter ball inside the old fish bag before dozing off again. On two separate occasions, however, the awakening was terrifying. Both times he was being buffeted about on the floor of the boat while it thumped and rasped and swirled in the darkness as it was swept through rapids. Had it been daylight and could he have seen and better comprehended what was occurring, he would have been even more afraid than he was. But in the darkness, drenched with the cold spray of river water, he simply kept his eyes squeezed shut and braced himself as best he could beneath the plank seat. Soon the bucking and bouncing ceased and the boat floated smoothly again in unobstructed waters.

When at last the final cascade was well behind him, he fell asleep again and was oblivious when, in the predawn darkness, his boat floated silently and unnoticed past the glinting campfires of the Metis. He was still asleep when, just as dawn fractured the eastern sky, the boat drifted out of the river's mouth and into the vast expanse of Lake Winnepeg.

Not until the sun appeared and twinkled as a million sparkling points of light off the faintly rippled surface did he stir and stretch his cramped limbs. He groaned as he squirmed out from beneath the seat, and then he kicked the bag off and sat up. His jaw dropped and he stared in wonderment at what he saw. To the north and east there was nothing but water. Westward the shore dwindled and finally disappeared as it began curving northward. To the south, the shoreline trees, well over a mile distant, were visible only as an ill-defined line of dark conifers with picket-pointed tops, that line gradually disappearing into the horizon to the southeast. Never before in his short life had he seen so vast a body of water, and it both thrilled and frightened him.

The river current that had carried him out so far had dissipated to a large extent in the broadness of the lake, and the generally westward drift of the boat was now all but imperceptible. Once again he went to the bow, where he first scooped up some water in his cupped hand and drank it and then began paddling with both hands. This time he noted with satisfaction that the bulky boat was actually beginning to move with his efforts. He headed south at first, toward the closest point of the shoreline, but the sun's brilliance slanting off the water to the left front so pained his eyes that he turned to a more southwestern heading. It would be a little farther, but at least there was no glare.

Ben's ambition exceeded his capabilities. Before long his hands and arms became so cold from the water that they ached all the way up to his elbows and again exhaustion was overtaking him. He stopped and returned to the center seat, where he sat down facing the southwestern shoreline, his hands pressed tightly between his thighs in an effort to warm them. He had no idea what would happen to him now, and he simply sat there in a sort of vacuum, detached from his surroundings.

Because of the exertion of paddling, he was no longer quite so chilled as before, but he was very hungry.

When a large fish swirled at the surface near the boat, he thought of how wonderful a big serving of crisply fried fish would taste. When a small flight of geese passed over him in a diagonal line, no more than a hundred feet above the water, he thought of the fine goose his mother had roasted for Christmas dinner last December and then morosely wondered if, in fact, that had been the last Christmas dinner he was ever to have with his family. He thought of the individual members of the family then: his father, stubborn and demanding, yet also strong and caring, and whom he loved so much; his mother, gentle and patient, warm and kind, and always interested in whatever Ben had to show or tell her; John, unfailingly protective of him, and who always listened to what he had to say; even Beth, studious and prissy though she was, would read to him the little poems she wrote that she allowed no one else to see and would tuck him in at bedtime, and kiss him lightly on the cheek when she thought he was asleep; and, finally, ten-year-old Coral, three years younger than Beth and three years older than he, everlastingly cheerful, bright, and funny, the perpetual flibbertigibbet who sometimes opened up to Ben, telling him her dreams and fears and hopes, and occasionally even crying as she related them. Oh, how he loved them all. And how deeply, desperately, he missed them now.

Again he let go and cried, his shoulders heaving with the sobs, until the sounds diminished to a whisper over the gently rippling water. At length there was no sound at all and he simply sat, elbows on knees, cheeks couched in hands, a minute lonely figure in a small boat in the vastness of a great body of water.

How long he remained sitting like that he had no idea, but the sun was much higher above the horizon when he gradually became aware of a movement in the distance between himself and the shoreline, a movement repeated in regular, rhythmic cadence. At first he thought it might be a swimming moose, like the one he had once seen crossing the Red River. He watched closely and then suddenly gasped aloud when at last it resolved itself into a canoe with a single occupant, heading directly toward him. A stab of fear lanced him as he realized it was an Indian. He was suddenly acutely aware of his utter defenselessness.

It took quite a while for the birch canoe to draw near. When it was only fifty feet or so distant, the Indian stopped paddling and let the light craft skim closer of its own momentum. Sitting on a pad on a raised seat slightly aft of center was a Metis youth who looked to be a year or so younger than John, perhaps fifteen or sixteen, his ebony hair in a single braid that was lying forward over one shoulder, its ribbon-tied end hanging halfway to his waist. The haft of a large knife projected from a brightly decorated sheath attached to his waistband. Barefoot and clad only in a soft, light-colored buckskin vest with frilled edging and an unadorned breechclout, also of buckskin, the Indian boy smiled hesitantly and bobbed his head. Raising one hand midchest high, palm forward, he spoke in a quiet voice.

"Kiyam api, napesis. Ekawiya sekisi. Namwatch ki ka mayitotatin." The words, spoken in the Cree language were, "Peace, little boy. Do not be afraid. I won't harm you."

The seven-year-old could not understand the strange words, but he sensed that the reassuring tone and the raised hand were friendly indications. He half-smiled in response, then raised his hand in the same sign and said, "Hello. I'm Ben. Who're you?"

The Metis youth cocked his head and smiled more broadly, but it was apparent that he understood Ben no more than Ben understood him. He didn't need to understand Ben's words, however, to tell that this little boy was in serious trouble and needed help. The canoe was about twenty feet distant from the rowboat now and angling slightly to one side, but a skillful dip of the paddle put it back on course and sent it directly alongside Ben's boat.

Inside the trim craft, a couple of feet in front of the young man, was a crudely made bow and a few flint-tipped arrows fletched with sections of stiff quill feathers from a prairie chicken. It didn't appear to be much of a weapon, but that impression was belied by the freshly killed quarry that lay close by: a large green-headed duck, a fat porcupine, and a snowshoe hare with its mottled coat indicative that it was in the midst of changing from its winter snowsuit to summer tans. Since the canoe had approached Ben from the southwest, it seemed evident that the youth had been hunting along that shore this morning, and rather skillfully at that.

As the two boats touched, the young Indian firmly gripped the rowboat's gunwale and indicated with hand signs that Ben should get into the canoe toward the front. Despite lingering fears, it seemed to Ben a more reasonable choice than staying in the rowboat, so he nodded and did so, climbing in slowly and carefully so as not to tip the delicate craft, gripping its sides to steady himself and immediately settling himself firmly and with good balance.

The rope with which the rowboat had been tied to the tree still trailed into the water off the bow, and Ben assumed the Metis was going to tie it to the stern of his canoe and tow it behind. He was dismayed when, as soon as he was settled, the boy shoved away from it and left the cumbersome wooden craft to drift on, abandoned.

"That's my father's boat," Ben protested. "I can't just let it go."

The Indian shook his head and resumed paddling, smiling gently whenever Ben glanced back to look at the rowboat diminishing on the lake's surface behind them. With strong, smooth strokes that produced surprising speed, the youth set a course toward the southeast. After several minutes, when Ben swiveled around to look back, the Metis paused in his steady stroking and, as if something had just occurred to him, lay his paddle aside.

Ben watched curiously as he reached back and retrieved a soft, tanned leather pouch from behind him, then opened its flap and reached inside. He extracted a half-inch-thick slab of something shaped roughly like a rectangle about five or six inches long and a couple of inches wide. He extended it toward Ben, but the little boy, having no idea what it was and leery of it, drew back. The Indian youth laughed aloud at Ben's reaction. He lifted the rectangle to his mouth, fastened his strong white teeth into one corner, then bit off a chunk and chewed with apparent relish. He swallowed the bite and again extended the slab toward Ben, pointing to it with his free hand.

"Pemmican," he said. *"Pemmican."*

Still with some hesitation, Ben accepted it and looked at it carefully. It was a dense material, brownish but mottled with bits of white, red, and black. Hunger was strong in him, but still he was cautious. He lifted it closer to his nose and sniffed at it tentatively. It had a smell that was reminiscent of the distinctive but not unpleasant aroma that arose when his mother rendered beef fat to make lard. He glanced at the Indian, who grinned again, nodded, and then patted his own stomach encouragingly.

Gingerly, Ben nibbled a small bite off one of the corners and began to chew it. The texture was similar to that of some of the medium-soft candy his mother made, but it was not sweet. The flavor was wonderful, with a sort of beefy-fruity taste, and quickly he took another bite, considerably larger than the first.

"Good!" he exclaimed enthusiastically, speaking around the mouthful of food even though he knew it to be bad manners. "Good," he repeated, and extended the slab back toward the Metis boy. The latter shook his head and raised his hand, palm down, level with his mouth, indicating that he was full, then motioned for Ben to continue eating, which he did.

The Metis pointed at himself. *"Niya Apistchi-Paskwawi-Mustus,"* he said, tapping his chest with his index finger — I am Little Buffalo. *"Niya. Ni wiyowin. Apistchi-Paskwawi-Mustus nit'isihikasun."* Me. My name. My name is Little Buffalo. He said it again slowly, *"Apistchi-Paskwawi-Mustus."*

"Ah-peest-chee pass-kwa-wee mooz-tus," Ben parroted phonetically, his mouth forming the unfamiliar words awkwardly. He tapped his own chest. "Ben. My name is Ben."

"Ben," the Metis said, mimicking the word exactly. He pointed at himself again and said, *"Apistchi-Paskwawi-Mustus,"* then pointed at the boy and said, "Ben."

Suddenly they were both laughing. They had communicated! Ben felt proud of himself at the achievement and assumed the Metis boy felt the same. As Little Buffalo started to paddle again and Ben continued eating the pemmican, they tried other words.

The nouns were easiest. In turn the young Indian indicated various things nearby and spoke the name in the Cree tongue. *Atchapiy* was the "bow," and *akask* was "arrow." The porcupine was *kakwa,* the snowshoe hare was *wapus-asam,* and the duck was *sisip.* It became something of a game, and with each identification the older boy made in Cree, Ben not only repeated the Indian term but also concentrated on committing it to memory, and then said the name of the same thing in English, which Little Buffalo similarly memorized.

When Ben finished off the slab of pemmican, he was still hungry, and Little Buffalo dug again into his pouch — which he identified as *pittasuwinis* — and withdrew another and gave it to Ben, who munched it with pleasure. The first verb he learned was "eat," which was *mitchisu*, although, thinking about it, Ben reasoned the word *Apistchi-Paskwawi-Mustus* told him might as easily have been "chew." There was little doubt with the second verb, however, when Ben pointed at his own throat, swallowed a bite in an exaggerated manner, and said, "Swallow." Grinning, the Indian lad made a dry swallow and said, "*Kutchipayitta.*" Again, it struck them both as funny and they laughed heartily together.

The word game continued to keep them occupied while the trim little craft sliced through the placid waters toward the shore, which was now considerably closer. The paddle, Little Buffalo said, was *apuiy*, but the act of paddling was an entirely different word — *pimiskawin* — and the canoe itself turned out to be *tchiman*. The Metis fingered his own hair and gave the Cree designation for that — *mistakay* — and then did the same with vest, breechclout, knife, sheath, nose, eye, mouth, tongue, teeth, ear, cheek, chin, arm, hand, foot, leg, and chest, which were, in turn, *papakiweyan, mitas, mokuman, pitchikumanan, miskiwan, miskisik, miton, miteyaniy, manaway, mikaskunew, mispitun, mitchitchiy, misit, miskat, miskik, miskaska,* and *maskigan*. Ben thought it strange that all these various body parts began with the letter *m* but he was unable to ask why this was so.

Caught up in this game of naming things, Little Buffalo, failing to find anything else in the canoe to identify, pointed at the sun and said, *"Kisikawipisim,"* then pointed to a big, puffy cloud, which he called *"waskow."*

The verbs continued to be a little more difficult. "Water" was *nipiy*, but "drink" was *minikwewin*. "See" turned out to be *wapattamowin*, while *pettamowin* was "hear," or perhaps "listen." At one point Ben, embarrassed, abruptly had to relieve himself, and he carefully stood up, his back to the paddler, and urinated over the side. As he did so, Little Buffalo, behind him said, *"Siki,"* and Ben went into such gales of laughter that it was a wonder he didn't fall overboard or upset the canoe, his mirth occasioned by the fact that he didn't know whether *siki* meant what he was doing or what he was holding. They did not cease identifying things and parroting each other until they neared shore.

The mouth of the Red River was now off to their right—westward—about a half-mile distant, with a sizable village barely visible closer to the river's mouth. But directly ahead of them was a smaller village made up of largely identical log huts. Each was about twenty feet square, the logs notched at the ends to interlock and the flat roofs made of saplings that had been stripped of branches and tied parallel to one another across the top, then covered with broad pieces of bark weighted down and sealed with squares of sod. The huts were built roughly in a circle around a somewhat larger, similarly built structure. Numerous canoes were beached along the gently sloped shoreline, and it was toward the midst of these that they were headed.

A few people had gathered at the shore, and as the canoe approached, more were coming until quite a crowd had assembled and stood waiting. A ripple of renewed fear spread over Ben. Little Buffalo was still smiling, and he had been kind to him, but he was just an older boy. What about these people? Schoolyard rumors of atrocities committed by the Indians came back in a rush, filling Ben's mind with gruesome pictures, and the ripple of fear became a wave.

When the canoe scraped ashore and the two boys disembarked, there arose a great chatter of conversation that was incomprehensible to Ben and which sounded menacing to him. All of the men and even some of the women wore sheathed knives, and here and there were individuals with bows or rifles. He mistook their curiosity about him as threatening and, as they pressed closer to him, he began to tremble and only through great effort managed to keep from bursting into tears. When one or two of those who were closest reached out to touch him, he cringed, and was inordinately relieved when Little Buffalo stepped close and put an arm about him protectively.

What followed was a blur of activity that became very confusing to Ben. As the center of a group, with a horde of shrieking, laughing children and barking dogs racing madly about, he was led by Little Buffalo toward the larger structure. Inside was a single expansive room into which the people crowded. Its slightly raised center was dominated by a rock-rimmed fire site in which no fire glowed at the moment. He was shown to a number of men who were apparently chieftains, though they looked little different from the other men, who stood back respectfully.

Little Buffalo, obviously proud of being part of the center of attention, spoke at length, and Ben could only assume he was telling them of how he saved the little white boy adrift without oars and far from shore in the expanse of Lake Winnipeg. The listeners nodded and smiled, and occasionally individuals murmured briefly to one another.

Several of the principal men addressed questions to Ben directly, speaking first in the Cree tongue and then in French, neither of which he could understand, nor could he make a response. One of the men indicated Little Buffalo and Ben in the same gesture and spoke authoritatively for a short while. It seemed he was putting the white boy in Little Buffalo's charge. On the heels of that, the lead man summoned forward from the crowd a man and woman, whom Little Buffalo greeted warmly. Ben needed no interpreter to correctly deduce that these were his companion's parents. When they indicated that he should follow them, he did so without hesitation, and they took him to one of the smaller huts.

Inside that structure they made him comfortable, and it was then that Little Buffalo identified his father as *Ka Papamuttet-Moswa* and his mother as *Ka Sipika-kwapikwaniy ka paskapikwanet*. Ben, after a few tries that brought laughter to the listeners, was able to phonetically repeat the father's name as "kah pah-pah-moot-tay mah-swah" and the mother's long name as "kah see-peek-ah-kwah-pee-kwah-ny-ee kah pah-skah-pee-kwah-nay," but it was to be quite a while before he realized that the names translated to Walking Moose and Blue Flower Opening. The latter served him hot tea—and he was delighted to find that "tea" was the same in both languages—in a slightly battered pewter cup and rich soup—*mitchimapuiy*—in a wooden bowl, followed by an excellent stew—

pakatchiwasuwin—which contained succulent chunks of well-cooked meat. Despite having eaten the pemmican earlier, he eagerly devoured what they gave him, and Little Buffalo joined him in the meal.

For some time afterward, they sat together and attempted to converse, but Ben's ability with the Cree language was still so limited that it became pointless for the time being. Besides, even though it was now only a little after midday, he was very sleepy, the accumulation of frightening experiences, physical effort, and an overpowering wave of new impressions having exhausted him, to say nothing of the fear of what might lie ahead, which continued to haunt him. Recognizing this, they led him to a comfortable bed of densely furred buffalo hide and pulled a warm woolen trade blanket over him. Then they went away.

It felt so good to Ben to stretch out like this, at least momentarily safe and warm and well fed. He sighed contentedly, but the contentment did not last. His churning thoughts turned to his situation, and he was jolted back to the reality that while he was apparently not a prisoner, nor in any way treated as such—at least not yet—perhaps this was all just an illusion to put him off-guard until they could deal with him in a more harsh manner, as he had initially feared. Maybe they meant to torture him, as the stories he had heard described, by carving him up into little pieces to feed to their dogs. Or maybe they meant to tie him to a stake and burn him. The thoughts frightened him, and he tried to thrust them away, but they continued to plague him. Even if they just kept him prisoner, without physically harming him, that would mean that he might never see home again. The thought brought tears to his eyes, and he suddenly found himself silently crying.

No! He was not going to act like a baby about all this. He wiped away the tears with the heel of his hand and made a decision to try to deal with his present situation in a more positive manner. That, however, was easier thought than done; the possibility of never seeing home again triggered thoughts of his family and how deeply he missed them and how they, too, must be frantic with worry over him. He wished there were some way he could assure them he was still all right. But that was not possible. With an effort he pushed down the thought that even if he were able to get away from these people, he had no idea how—or even *if*—he could get home. It was up to him, somehow, some way, to get back home, and he resolved now that he would. He had to return to Hawk's Hill. He *had* to.

CHAPTER 4

For three days the MacDonald family —
particularly William and John — searched extensively
for Ben, but the only thing they found was consistent
disappointment.

On the day of the disappearance, the elder Mac-
Donald and his son had gotten back to Hawk's Hill
from Lower Fort Garry long after nightfall, their dejec-
tion made even deeper by having to face Ben's mother
and sisters with the news that the little boy had not
been found. By dawn's first light the following morning, the five of them had all gone out to the first knoll
south of Hawk's Hill, to the exact spot where Ben had

alighted from the buggy. Using this as the focal point, and maintaining an arm's-length distance apart, they walked soberly side by side in an ever-widening circle through the lush, knee-high grasses, eyes probing and searching the ground cover for any trace whatever of Ben's passage. All were keenly aware that if they found anything, it might turn out to be his body, but they had to look, had to know.

Their circling gradually widened, and after a few hours the girls became too tired to continue. At their mother's bidding, the pair returned to the buggy, where they sat huddled together on the seat, watching their parents and John continue the methodical search. On and on the three went in the ever-broadening pattern until its eastern perimeter reached the river's edge and the northern perimeter was at the crest of the hill. Still no trace.

When they paused at the top to rest for a little while, John stared at their distant house and barn perched atop Hawk's Hill and suddenly shook his head. "I don't think he would've come any farther this way," he said. "What if he heard me yell like I did? What if he heard Coral and Beth screaming? If he did, maybe it scared him so much he ran straight out into the prairie. He probably wouldn't've run toward the river 'cause he'd have known he couldn't get far that way.

So" — he shrugged — "maybe if we go straight west from the road, we'll have a better chance. I don't know." He shrugged again.

His parents considered this quietly, and then William nodded. "You might have something there, John. It's worth a try, anyway. Esther, why don't you take the girls and go up to the house and get a bite to eat? John and I will head out westward from the road and start ranging that way."

They did so, but later, when Esther came out with sandwiches and milk for them, they had zigzagged fully a quarter mile from the road without finding a scrap of evidence that Ben had gone that way. By this time, several neighbors on horseback had shown up and were aiding in the search, as were half a dozen soldiers — a squad from the fort under command of a sergeant — and so considerably more of the prairie was combed. By twilight they had extended the pattern fully a mile into the prairie, and still there was no trace.

In the evening the five MacDonalds sat somberly around the dinner table and again discussed where they should check next. With no evidence of Ben or his passage having yet been found, William was more than ever convinced that no other possibility existed than that George Burton had crested the hill and spotted Ben running away, then had ridden him down, caught him, and carried him off.

Therefore, the next morning, despite a persistent drizzle falling, father and son once again rode toward North Corners and searched closely for where Burton might have left the road. Light though the rain was, however, it was enough to obliterate the traces they sought, and they again returned home in the evening, weary and more dejected than ever. Scattered search parties from North Corners and Lower Fort Garry had been checking their areas, too, similarly without success. Ben—and Burton, too, for that matter—seemed simply to have vanished, and the fact that neither had been found seemed more than reasonable evidence for linking these two disappearances into one occurrence.

The next morning, the third morning of their search for Ben, all the MacDonald family members were feeling the strain of their fruitless efforts. They were running out of ideas of what to do, of where to look next, and so they spent the first part of the day closely checking areas that they had initially ignored—places that had seemed too improbable to consider when the searching began. A thorough search was made of the barn—and even their own house—with the idea that perhaps Ben had been hurt and had managed to make his way back home and hide himself before passing out. Again, nothing. Then, as they rested and had lunch, it was ten-year-old Coral who came up with a new theory. Being so young and seldom able to contribute much of value, and always with a distinct flair for the dramatic, she broached the idea in a roundabout way.

"Maybe I've figured out what happened," she murmured.

"Oh, sure!" Beth snorted. "No one else can figure out what happened, but you think you know." She giggled and then added scornfully, "I'll just bet you do."

"Beth, enough!" Esther warned. She was pale and drawn with the strain of the past days, and so far as she was concerned, any possibility at this point was worth listening to. She turned to her younger daughter. "Go on, dear."

"Well," Coral said, pleased that she now had everyone's attention, "I was trying to put myself in Ben's place and figure what I would do if I was him."

"Were," Esther corrected her automatically. She seemed abruptly appalled at her own triviality under these circumstances but went on nonetheless. "If I *were* him. It's the subjunctive mode."

"Okay, were," Coral amended. "If I were Ben and I heard us girls screaming like we did"—she broke off and corrected herself before anyone else could—"*as we did*, I think I would probably have run up to the top of the hill to see what was going on."

"We checked the top of the hill, and he wasn't there," Beth reminded her.

"Well, let me finish!" Coral protested. "Mama, tell her . . ."

"Beth," her mother said sternly, "no more now. That's the last warning."

"Go on, honey," her father said, reaching across the table and patting Coral's arm. He had, however, already discounted whatever it might be that she was going to say. What theory could a ten-year-old advance that they had not already considered?

Shooting a triumphant glance at her elder sister, Coral continued, her brow wrinkling as she gathered her thoughts. "Okay, so he gets to the top and he sees us, but he sees Mr. Burton, too. What does he do? Well, since he sees John galloping us home as fast as we can go, he probably hides in some bushes and waits until Mr. Burton goes past on his horse. Then, instead of jumping up and running, when maybe he could still be seen, he sneaks through the grass to the nearest cover he can find." She paused.

"Which is?" her father nudged.

"Which is the trees along the river. When he gets

there and is hidden from Mr. Burton's view, he runs downstream along the shore to where your old boat is tied up."

"The boat!" John cried and leaped to his feet so quickly his chair tipped over backward. "We never even thought of that, Papa! I'll check it out."

He raced out of the house, and a moment later they heard hoofbeats as he galloped his horse toward the river. William leaned over and set the chair upright, shaking his head. "It's a good thought, Coral," he said, "but it's not very likely. As you know, I've warned him—all of you, in fact—over and over never *ever* to get into that boat alone, so I doubt he'd even think about going there."

"But under these circumstances, William," Esther put in, grasping at the straw of hope Coral had just given them, "maybe it's not so far-fetched an idea. And even if he didn't go to the boat, what if he just ran north as Coral suggests and kept going until he was safe? We only searched to the west, east, and south."

William continued shaking his head through all of this. "If that were the case, why wouldn't he have come straight home as soon as it was safe for him to do so? It just doesn't make any sense."

"What if . . . ," Beth began, then broke off, shaking her head.

"What if what, honey?" her mother urged. "C'mon, bring it out. We have to consider any possibility."

Now Beth was reluctant to go on, but she did so, hesitantly, lowering her eyes as she spoke. "Well, what if he ran straight east to the edge of the river to hide there, but fell in. He's not a very good swimmer and . . . and . . ." Her voice trailed off as she was unable to finish the thought. Suddenly she was crying, and Esther got up and put her arms around the girl.

Though she soothed her daughter, Esther's eyes were haunted because the same frightening thought had occurred to her more than once, and she and William had discussed this very possibility late at night after the children were asleep.

"It *is* something that has to be considered, Beth," she murmured, "but your father and I have talked about this, and we can only trust in God and believe that He would not have allowed such a thing to happen, that He would have given Ben the good sense to keep away from the water."

"Your mother and I decided," William put in, reaching over and stroking Beth's hair comfortingly, "that while such a possibility might exist, we had to believe in our hearts that it didn't occur. If all else fails," he added, his voice becoming less steady, "then John and I will make a search of the riverbank all the way down. But for now, Beth, you have to be strong and believe, as your mother and I do, that such a thing simply did not—"

He abruptly broke off as the sound of drumming hooves reached them and they heard John's voice faintly rising above the din. "Papa! Papa! *Mama!*"

There was such an unusual quality in the voice that the four very nearly knocked one another over in their rush to the porch. They watched with wildly rising hopes as John thundered up and reined in his horse with a swirl of dust and scattered clods of dirt.

"The boat's gone, Papa!" John exclaimed. "It's not there. And there was a deep footprint in the mud at the shoreline. A *small* footprint, Mama. Ben's!"

William snatched up Esther in a giant hug, lifting her clear off her feet, and Coral was jumping up and down in excitement, but this sudden bubble of jubilation surging through them all did not last. It was punctured by Beth.

"If Ben got away in the boat," she said nervously, "then how come he didn't row to shore as soon as it was safe and come home?"

Her father smacked his own forehead with his palm. "The oars," he groaned.

"What about them, Papa?" It was John. "Ben knows how to use them. I taught him."

"They weren't in the boat." William felt Esther stiffen in his grasp, and he let her go. "The wood in the blades was starting to split, and I brought them up to the barn to fix them if I could, or get some new ones if I couldn't." He shook his head. "They're still in there."

"Oh, dear God!" Esther exclaimed, her hand to her mouth and eyes wide in consternation.

Even as the others looked at her, she suddenly paled and swayed. William immediately put a steadying arm around her, but all of them knew exactly what she was envisioning: the powerful current of the Red River, the perilous rapids with thundering water and crushing rocks where a boat could easily be flipped over even when skillfully handled, the villages of the savage, rebellious Metis near the river's mouth, and, beyond all these, the dangerous vastness of Lake Winnipeg itself. How could tiny little Ben have survived any one of these, much less all?

There was no longer any question about what needed to be done. Wasting no time, William and John gathered up the necessaries and prepared their horses, both big strong geldings, while Esther filled a pouch with enough victuals to last them a couple of days. During a moment when they were alone together, William put his arms around Esther and held her close for a moment. Then he pulled back, his expression very sober, and spoke in a grim tone.

"I think I ought to leave John here. He can handle

himself and a gun very well. That's just in case Burton should show up here again."

Esther had already considered that possibility, and she shook her head. "No. You'll need him to help search for traces of Ben more than we'll need him here. Besides, I'm a good shot, too, remember? You ought to; it was you who taught me. We've still got the shotgun and the small rifle. If George Burton dares to show up here, he'll rue the day."

Esther sensed William's objection coming, and she shushed him with her fingertips pressed to his lips. "Don't argue," she said softly. "The girls and I will be fine—I promise. Just go! We're wasting time."

Actually, Esther wanted desperately to go with them, but with two young daughters to care for, it was obvious she could not. She wept as she kissed her husband and son good-bye and whispered to each, "Find him. Find our little Ben."

With misgivings still strong in William at leaving Esther and the girls alone, father and son rode out. When they reached the river and decided to follow the watercourse downstream, both realized that, ideally, there should be a rider on each side in case the boat had come ashore on the opposite bank. At the same time they recognized the foolhardiness of trying to swim a horse across at this point of the broad, swift river. With the nearest relatively safe crossing eight miles upstream, at Dunblane's Ferry near North Corners, they grimly settled on remaining on this west side, but they would keep a sharp eye on the far shore as well.

Because of the denseness of the riverine growth and the close attention they were paying to the ground for any sign of tracks, they moved slowly. Though neither of them admitted to doing so, each was also closely scanning the water's edge for the terrible possibility they did not want to put into words.

Nightfall overtook them about a mile before they reached the river's mouth. In the dubious shelter they found between a couple of large wind-fallen trees, they made a cold camp, fearful that if they built a fire, even a very small one, it would be seen by the Metis and they would risk being attacked in the darkness. They huddled close together under their blankets. It was an uncomfortable night for them, but neither complained, realizing that for Ben, assuming he was still alive, it had to be much worse.

At dawn they were again mounted and moving downstream. They had encountered not a single trace of any person by the time they reached the head of Lake Winnipeg at sunrise. Keeping as much under brushy cover as they could to avoid being seen, they could make out, directly across the broad mouth of the river, which here was close to one hundred yards wide, one of the several Metis villages said to be located at this strategic site. This one fronted on both the river and the lake. Smoke wafted lazily upward from what log huts were visible, but only about a dozen Indians could be seen moving about. As far as they could tell, all were women, some of whom were going down to the shoreline, where the canoes were beached, bottoms up, and filling their jugs with water, which they carried back to the dwellings.

"Papa," John whispered, "if Ben somehow managed to get through the rapids safely, maybe they saw the boat drifting past and went out in their canoes and brought it in. Maybe we should just figure out how to get over there and ride in and make some queries."

"Not a good idea, son," his father whispered back without hesitation. "At least not yet. If the boat did make it through the rapids safely, figuring the speed of the current and all, it would almost certainly have floated past here sometime during the night and there'd be little chance it was seen."

"But what if they *did* happen to see it?" John persisted. "It's got to at least be a possibility."

William remained silent for a moment, staring through the foliage at the distant village. At last he shook his head. "John, from where we are right here, we can see both whole shorelines of that village, the river side and the lake side. Lots of canoes drawn up on shore but not a trace of the old rowboat. It's a lot heavier than any of those canoes, so it's unlikely, if they did bring it in, that it wouldn't be there with the canoes. Since it's not, its far more likely that it drifted through in the darkness without being seen. Also, these savages have been becoming more hostile every passing day, and for us to boldly show up in their village would be asking for trouble, even though we were to come to them peacefully. You just can't trust a Half-Breed, John."

"But—"

The elder MacDonald cut off his son's remark with a sharply upraised hand. "Furthermore," he continued, "do you see how the river curves a good bit westward right here at the point where it empties into the lake? That means the river current would continue to carry a drifting boat more to the west and maybe slightly north than to the northeast, over in front of the village. If the boat made it through, then it probably drifted over that way somewhere." Again he indicated the shore they were on, but far ahead, where it began its gradual curve to the northwest. "And where it came ashore is where Ben, if he were still in it, would have climbed out. We've got to follow this shore westward to where it starts heading north. God willing, we'll find the boat. And Ben."

Still with a degree of reluctance, John nodded. "All right, Papa. Let's go, then."

Throughout the remainder of the day, they rode west, always watching the shoreline closely for the boat and equally studying the ground ahead for any footprint or other trace that a small boy's passage might have left. They saw numerous ducks paddling in little inlets, as well as a great blue heron standing silent sentinel in a marshy shallow on its long thin legs, patiently awaiting a fish to swim past that would become its next meal. Several large flights of geese passed by overhead, their impressive V formations splitting the sky on this final leg of their northern migration from a thousand miles or more to the south. At one point a large black bear, startled by their approach, nearly panicked the horses by bursting from dense cover mere yards ahead of them before quickly disappearing in the dense pine forest that came close to the lake. On another occasion they saw a huge bull moose standing belly-deep in the water of a small pond, feeding on the floating foliage of water lilies. A pair of bulbous, velvet-covered growths sprouting from its head gave promise of the massive spread of antlers they would grow into by autumn. Here and

there they saw porcupines climbing in trees or wad-
dling unconcernedly along on the ground. They
glimpsed a wolf carrying the limp carcass of a snowshoe hare in its teeth and guessed it was a female taking prey to her pups at some well-hidden den. But of
the object of their search, they saw nothing.

By the time the sun had slipped down through the
western sky until it was only a few degrees over the
western horizon, they had already swum their horses
across many small creeks and two streams entering the
lake from the south and were now well into following
the broad curve where the shoreline began heading
north. Dejected though they felt, they agreed to ride
until sunset, probably another twenty minutes, before
stopping for the night. Then, tomorrow morning, if no
trace of Ben or the boat were found after a brief search,
they would head homeward.

They encountered a reasonable little trail—whether
animal or Indian, they couldn't be certain—that paral-
leled the shore in sight of the waterline, and they followed it, making the ride much easier on their horses.
When it was close to sunset and William was half dozing in the saddle, a sudden excited outburst from his
son jerked him stiffly alert.

"Papa! The boat—there it is. We found it!"

William's gaze followed the direction of John's
pointing finger, and then he saw it, too. The old

wooden rowboat was wedged in the branches of a giant pine that had long ago toppled into the lake when its roots had become undermined by the lapping of waves. Their blood suddenly surging in excitement, they quickly rode in as close as they could, tied their horses, and then climbed up on the sloping trunk and followed it outward and downward as close as they could to the boat.

John was silently fearful that they would find his little brother's body in the bottom of the craft, but when they looked down into it, he breathed a sigh of relief. Except for an old rumpled cloth sack, it was empty. They surmised that when the boat had wedged itself here, Ben had scrambled through the limbs and made it to shore, so they checked all the branches carefully, as well as the immediate shoreline in a thirty-foot semicircle around the tree. They found nothing.

"Just because we haven't found any sign of him doesn't mean he wasn't in the boat when it got here, Papa," John said as they paused near the waterline. "Look, he probably didn't jump off the trunk here where it's soft. He probably followed it all the way up to the root clump and got down there, where the ground's harder."

"Maybe, John. Maybe." But William was far from convinced. Ever since determining that the boat was empty, he had been plagued by the devastating thought that Ben may have been thrown out of the boat as it passed through the turbulent waters of the Red River rapids.

With twilight upon them, they made their second night's camp in a little glade well above the waterline and the wedged boat. At William's insistence, it was again a cold camp, though both father and son would have greatly welcomed a fire to brew some tea. Instead, they gnawed strips of jerky and hard biscuits from their much-dwindled food supply. As they ate these meager rations, they discussed the possibilities that it was now necessary for them to consider in order to formulate a course of action for the morrow.

"Here's the situation as I see it," the elder Mac-Donald said. He began ticking off his remarks on his fingers as he made them, starting with the thought that had been bothering him so much. "First, we have to admit that it's quite possible Ben was thrown out of the boat when it went through the rapids."

"If that's what happened, Papa," John said softly, "then he certainly would have drowned. He just can't swim all that well, and it wouldn't have been possible for him to fight that current."

William nodded. "I agree." He was silent for a few heartbeats, and then he ticked off another finger.

"Second, as we previously discussed, he could have been taken by the Metis, and they could have just let the empty boat drift on."

"Which makes it still a possibility for us to check out if everything else fails."

Again William murmured an agreement and went on: "Third, if he stayed with the boat to here, he could have fallen in and drowned while he was attempting to climb through that slanted tree." When John said nothing, he continued. "Fourth, if indeed he reached the shore safely after climbing through the tree, there's a reasonable likelihood that he was disoriented and didn't know which way to go. In that case, he might have wandered off and really become lost, and the likelihood of finding him then would be zero, unless he marked his trail. Fifth and finally, if he were keen enough to do so, he may have figured out which way to go to reach Hawk's Hill and started off in that direction."

"So what do we do now, Papa?"

"In the morning we'll make a search. We'll separate. You head north and range back and forth in an arc from the shoreline due west. I'll try south, ranging the same way. Watch closely for any sign whatever that Ben may have left—footprints, bent branches, broken twigs, anything. I'll do the same. If one of us finds any definite sign, he fires three spaced shots to alert the other to come at once. If we haven't discovered anything by noon, we'll meet right back here and start heading for home, zigzagging a little as we go on the chance we can pick up Ben's trail. We've got enough food left for a bite to eat in the morning, and that's about it. Maybe we'll be able to bag a duck or a raccoon or something on the way back. If not, we're going to be mighty hungry by the time we reach Hawk's Hill." He paused and yawned. "Well, I guess that covers it. Let's get some sleep now. We'll need to be well rested."

By this time full darkness was upon them, and they suddenly became pleased with themselves for not having built even a small fire, as they had so much wished to do. From far over the dark waters to the southeast of them, bright pinpoints of light were shining — the campfires of the Metis villages.

A little later still, as they lay side by side under their blankets with their guns close at hand, William stared up at the midnight blue canopy of the sky peppered with a myriad of tiny twinkling stars. He wondered if his little son were still alive somewhere and if they would ever find him. He thought of John, too, and of how much help the seventeen-year-old had been over these past four days of searching, and all the hardships he had endured without one word of complaint. Abruptly the stars above blurred as a welling of pride arose in him and a mistiness filled his eyes. He rolled over, closer to his son, and laid his hand on the boy's head, stroking his hair gently. Then he leaned even closer and softly kissed his cheek.

"I love you, son," he whispered. He rolled back and pulled the blanket snugly around his neck. Again he stared at the star-studded darkness above and realized with something of a shock that he couldn't remember the last time he had kissed his eldest son or told him that he loved him.

Neither could John.

CHAPTER 5

The little village of Maskwa on the southernmost shore of Lake Winnipeg was the smallest of five Metis villages clustered within a mile or so of one another on the east side of the Red River's mouth. Three others, not much larger, were Sasaginnigan, Wanipagow, and Koostatak, a bit more distant from the lake. The principal village, as well as the largest, was Singush. A small portion of this latter village was what William and John had glimpsed when they had peered through the foliage on the other side of the river.

It was to Singush that Ben MacDonald was being

escorted by Little Buffalo and his parents, Walking Moose and Blue Flower Opening, on this sixth day of his stay with them. From their actions, he surmised that something important was about to occur, and wondered if their chief had returned.

The preceding five days with the Metis had provided revelations of considerable significance to the white boy. He and Little Buffalo had strolled about at length in two of the villages, Maskwa and its nearest neighbor, Koostatak, and while Ben was the object of many curious glances, he was in no manner threatened or bothered by anyone. The fears that he had harbored of the Metis quickly dissolved.

Ben was more than a little amazed to discover that, on the whole, the Metis were a happy, good people, quick to laughter and amazingly industrious. Everyone, even the children, seemed to have specific tasks to do, and they engaged in them with an enthusiasm and vigor that made it clear they enjoyed and took pride in their work. When not so engaged, they became involved with equal enthusiasm in sports and games of wide variety. Family ties were very strong and became most apparent at evening time, when they would gather at their meal and afterward to discuss the day's events, listen to storytellers, sing their peculiarly appealing tribal songs, and dance to the cadence of strange but melodic musical instruments — reed pipes, skin drums, gourd rattles, lute-like stringed devices, and xylophonic sticks tapped together.

Highly impressive to Ben was the love these people constantly exhibited for one another and the respect, almost bordering on reverence, that they showed to the elderly. Witnessing all this, the boy could not help but experience a great pang of loneliness for his own family, and he realized more than ever before how much they meant to him. As nearly as Ben could gather from what Little Buffalo tried to tell him, the main chief of the Metis was away and was expected to return in a few days. At that time, he would be the one to decide what was to be done about Ben. The thought caused a resurgence of Ben's fears, though not quite so strongly as before, because of the obvious friendship that Little Buffalo and the other Metis were showering upon him.

During those days they had to wait for the return of the Metis leader, Little Buffalo, with great fervor and obvious enjoyment, undertook Ben's education in Metis ways and the Cree language, and he delighted in how quickly the little white boy learned. The first day, when he had been brought to the lodge of Little Buffalo's parents, Ben had slept most of the afternoon and all through the night. The second and third days, however, his young Metis rescuer had continued intensively instructing Ben in the native tongue. Ben's eager mind was like a thirsty sponge, rapidly absorbing and storing the words and their meanings. By the close of only his third day among the Metis, he had memorized a surprising number of Cree words and was even beginning to be able to string some of them together into simple sentences that, while decidedly ungrammatical, were certainly understandable.

However, Ben's involvement with the Cree language was only the beginning of what he was learning about the Metis culture. He was interested in everything about these people, and the more he saw, the more fascinating he found them to be. In many ways they were similar to white people, and yet in numerous other ways, they were remarkably different, and many of the impressions he had harbored about Indians before coming here were proving to be incorrect.

Because of the garb Little Buffalo had been wearing at their first encounter, Ben had assumed that all the Metis would be wearing similar leathers and furs, but such was not the case. For the most part, the clothing worn by these people was not that different from garb already familiar to him. Cotton, wool, and corduroy fabrics, acquired in trade, were common, and they favored bright colors. Ben watched with interest as one happily chatting circle of women and girls not only cut and sewed together shirts and blouses but also added armbands in which beads were strung in amazingly intricate geometric designs. Often the garments, especially for the men, were made of supple tanned hides of deer, elk, or moose, and beautiful fur cloaks fashioned from the pelts of beaver, martin, ermine, mink, fox, and lynx were also common. Although the children Ben saw went barefoot, most of the adults wore moccasins made from buffalo hide or moose leather, embellished with blue-, yellow-, and red-dyed porcupine quills.

The men rarely wore belts, choosing instead to hold up their woolen or skin trousers and leggings with broad, gaily decorated suspenders. They also favored an unusual item of clothing that was especially utilitarian. This was a broad sash, sometimes multicolored but more often bright scarlet, that was normally ten or twelve feet long but occasionally as much as twenty feet in length. Finger-woven by the women, these worsted sashes were wound by the men around the waist and sometimes looped over a shoulder. They not only provided warmth but also served as a useful rope when hauling canoes over portage places or whenever else a strong line was required.

The women were highly conscious of fashion and decorated their own clothing with beadwork, dyed quills, and brightly colored ribbons even more extensively than the men's. They wore pleated, puff-sleeved blouses tucked into full, ankle-length gathered skirts that were well ornamented with beadwork, silk threads, and ribbons. On cooler days, many of the women also wore colorful leggings of wool or velvet.

Ben was intrigued when he discovered that the Metis infants, called *papooses,* wore no clothes at all. Instead, they were carried about in an ingenious device called a *tikkinagan,* or *papoose* board—a cylindrical basket woven of cattail reeds or lithe willow switches, attached to a broad board and strapped to the mother's back. The interior of this device was one-third filled—and the inner sides well lined—with dense sphagnum moss that was frequently changed. The substance was not only soft and warm, but it also caught and absorbed the child's wastes and could be discarded and replaced in only a few moments. Ben was fascinated with how the women kept their babies with them at all times, and he was surprised by the fact that the *papooses* very rarely cried.

Blue Flower Opening showed Ben the type of food the Metis customarily ate and how it was prepared. The most important item was the meat of *mustus*— buffalo—which was regularly brought back to the villages by parties of skilled hunters that ranged the plains, following the great herds. All parts of the buffalo were used, none going to waste. Apart from the meat itself, the hide was very useful for robes, blankets, and footwear. Watertight bags were made from the stomach and intestines, and a thread that was almost impossible to break was derived from the long and stringy sinew running the length of the animal's back, which was dried and then separated into its individual strands. Even the hooves and horns were boiled down into a fine paste that made an excellent glue.

But while *mustus* meat was the mainstay of the Metis diet, many other staple meats were included: fowl such as ducks, geese, and prairie chickens—*sisipak, niskak,* and *pihyewok;* a wide variety of fish—*kinusew;* and abundant moose, elk, antelope, beaver, muskrat, and rabbit—*moswok, wawaskesiw, apistchimusus, kwaskuti-attikusis, watchask,* and *wapus.*

When berries were in season, the Metis dried and stored them in the buffalo-gut bags. Wild turnips were very important; when the pulp was dried and pounded into powder, it made a base for soup—the very soup, in fact, that Blue Flower Opening first fed to Ben on his arrival. Their principal bread, *gallette,* was closely akin to the traditional Scottish bread called bannock; it was hard, made of flour, water, lard, and baking powder, and could be kept for long periods.

Ben was able to observe Blue Flower Opening as she made the first Metis food he had ever tasted, pemmican, which could be kept for years without spoiling. She took long, thin strips of buffalo meat that had been sun-dried on willow racks and tied them inside a buffalo-gut bag, then pounded them vigorously with a heavy wooden pestle until they were pulverized into a powder. To this she added hot liquefied buffalo fat and mixed it well, then added a handful of chopped, dried blueberries and currants. Finally she molded it into a small pan, where it was left to congeal for several days. When she took it out, it was a flat rectangular cake.

There were so many sights and sounds, so many impressions to absorb, that Ben was nearly overwhelmed with it all, which was just as well; it helped prevent him from brooding over the separation from his family.

At first the Metis were merely amusedly impressed with the little white boy's efforts, but that swiftly changed. On the third day Ben was with them, the Indians suddenly began regarding him with profound astonishment. On that remarkable day, he and Little Buffalo, along with a group of other children and adults, took a walk through the woods bordering the lake shore.

A mile or so from Maskwa, the group encountered an area of rocks upthrusting through the soil, where numerous trees had long ago been knocked down by a severe storm. The result, which faced them now, was terrain that had become a difficult jumble, but they threaded their way through the chaos for some distance until they entered a small, relatively clear grassy area. Suddenly there came a weird sound that was part growl, part scream, and part snarl. Ben had never heard such a sound before, but it was apparent that at least some of the little group had.

"*Quiquihatch!*" one of the men shouted.

The Metis were instantly deeply alarmed. Most stood rooted in place, staring about fearfully, but a few started backing away toward the dubious shelter of the tangled, storm-downed trees. Little Buffalo and Ben were at the head of the group and closest to the frightening sound. The Metis youth immediately snatched the little white boy's arm and pulled at him, at the same time urgently echoing, "*Quiquihatch!*"

It was too late.

The hair-raising growl was abruptly augmented by the loud crackle of brittle branches snapping. These sounds originated from a sort of natural cavern some thirty feet distant across the little clearing. There, two massive trees had long ago fallen parallel to each other and lay sloped against a large emergent rock. Branches of other trees had fallen over them through the years until they had formed a sort of roof on the top and, underneath, a triangular cavity that was dark and forbidding. Almost inaudibly behind the more pronounced crackling and growling came squeaky little renditions of the same weird growling cry.

With startling suddenness a stocky, furry shape

lunged out of the darkness, its hideous snarling rising sharply in crescendo. In an instant the animal had covered more than half the distance to Ben and the group of Metis. While the boy was entranced by what was occurring, the Indians were petrified with fear. All of them were now assailed by a horrible stench emanating from the beast. No more than ten feet from Ben and Little Buffalo, it stopped, raised its head high, opened its mouth, and bared a fierce array of slightly yellowed fangs.

A multitude of impressions flashed through Ben's mind. At first glance, he thought the animal was a small bear, but just as quickly knew it was not. Remarkably heavily built and with a body about three feet long, the creature stood about a foot high at the shoulder. The bristling fur was long and extremely dense, blackish brown except for a band of paler brown low along its sides. Obviously very muscular and weighing at least thirty pounds, it had an exceptionally broad head, small rounded ears, and equally small malevolent eyes. Though Ben had never seen such an animal before in life, he had seen pictures of it in schoolbooks and had learned a good bit about it. He had always hoped that someday he would see one in the wild, and now he had.

It was a wolverine—the animal that the Indians of

most northern tribes held in superstitious awe. Some called it *carcajou,* but the Crees and Metis evidently knew it as *quiquihatch.* Because of its awful, permeating odor, many of the trappers called it a skunk bear, and because of its antagonistic behavior and deadly fighting abilities with both claws and teeth, others called it the Indian devil. But it was neither devil nor Indian, neither skunk nor bear. It was, in fact, the largest member of the weasel family in North America, ranking among the most fierce, surpassing even the well-known ferocity of its slightly smaller relative, the badger. Utterly fearless and particularly dangerous when cornered, this powerful animal was known to prey upon deer, caribou, and even bear, killing its victim by jumping on its back from an elevation and sinking those strong fangs into the neck. Stories were told that it also killed small moose and even young pumas—mountain lions—in this same manner.

Ben not only knew now that it was a wolverine and very dangerous under ordinary circumstances; he knew as well that this one before them was a decided threat to everyone here, because the present circumstances were hardly ordinary. This was an angry female, and the squeakier snarlings still faintly coming from the dark cavity were undoubtedly emanating from her litter. She would attack with unbelievable fury anything that she perceived as threatening them — and this was clearly her perception of the group of humans before her now.

Still snarling, she lowered her head slightly and crouched, and her muscles bunched as a prelude to springing into a charge at the nearest enemy—in this case, Little Buffalo. Then, incredibly, she paused as a new sound filled the clearing from directly in front of her, a sound almost identical to the squeaky snarlings from her offspring, but louder.

The sound was issuing from Ben and was an uncanny mimicry, embodying all the elements of fear, defiance, and plaintiveness uttered by the baby wolverines. Gradually moving past Little Buffalo, who stared aghast at him, the little boy repeated that odd mixture of high-pitched chirring, whining, and snarling as he slowly moved three steps closer to the wolverine.

Despite Ben's movement toward her, the big female *quiquihatch* visibly eased up from her attack posture, though she continued to watch the little boy intently. When the sound issued from him a third time, she ceased her own snarling and cocked her head in a puzzled way.

Remembering the time he had hand-fed some baby mice to a wild badger in the prairie last year, Ben now, as he continued making the sounds, sank slowly to one knee and leaned forward, putting his head almost on the same level as the wolverine's. At the same time, with no fast movements, he moved his right hand to his shirt pocket and removed an inch-square piece of pemmican he had saved to nibble on later. Still with the exaggeratedly slow movement, he gradually extended the tidbit until it was held out as far as he could reach, to within a foot of the wolverine. Behind him, Little Buffalo—and several yards behind him, the others—watched with open amazement. They hardly breathed as they witnessed something they would never forget.

The wolverine's teeth showed again briefly in a short-lived snarl, but then her bearlike nose wrinkled as she caught the scent of the pemmican. She remained as motionless as Ben for a long moment, her bristled fur gradually settling back into place, and then she slowly leaned forward. Unable to stretch far enough, she took three small hesitant steps and leaned forward again until her nose actually touched the tidbit. Then, with amazing delicacy considering her reputation, she cautiously licked the piece before gently fastening her teeth into it and pulling it from the boy's hand. For an instant more she stood there looking at him, her face level with his and the pemmican still protruding rather comically from her mouth.

Ben grinned and, withdrawing his extended arm,

made the chirring sound again. The wolverine continued staring into his face and then, uttering a little
chirp of her own, turned deliberately and seemed almost to flow back into the darkness of her lair. After a
moment more, Ben came back to his feet, walked
backward a few steps, and then turned and rejoined
the others. He was still grinning and, his eyes were
bright with the joy and excitement of his encounter.

As the group retraced its steps, the Metis regarded
Ben with awe. Little Buffalo was barely able to contain
the emotion that flooded him; he put an arm around
Ben's shoulders as they walked and hugged him
fiercely, certain now that his new young friend was especially endowed by the Great Spirit.

As they all headed back toward the village, Little
Buffalo and the others talked rapidly and excitedly
about what they had witnessed. To Ben, the entire
episode, while wonderful to have experienced, was not
really any great achievement on his part, and so,
though he could understand almost nothing of what
was being said, he merely smiled and nodded as they
regarded him with increased wonder. Once back in the
village, news quickly spread of what had occurred, and
Ben's education into the world of the Metis continued.

And now, at last, on this sixth morning of his stay
with the Metis, Ben and Little Buffalo and the youth's
parents had been summoned to the mile-distant prin-

cipal village, Singush. On the way, they strolled through fields and scattered woodlands, a large number of the villagers from Maskwa following at a respectful distance, hopeful, perhaps, of witnessing another amazing incident like that with the wolverine, but this time nothing unusual occurred. As they entered Singush, Ben could see that a sizable crowd had gathered there, far more than the large central council house could accommodate. Ben wondered what they were all standing around waiting for, and then, as the mass of people parted into an aisle, he realized it was for them. A niggling of fear came surging back but was quickly assuaged when he saw the friendliness in the expressions of those crowded around. Walking Moose and Blue Flower Opening, heads held proudly high, led the way toward the building's entry, while Little Buffalo and Ben walked side by side closely behind.

It took a moment for their eyes to adjust to the dimness inside, but gradually Ben could see that there was hardly room for another person. Those gathered in the interior sat on the earthen floor in a circular pattern around the central raised area, where a council fire glowed and where a man who was probably less than thirty years old stood waiting. He was clad in a black frock coat with matching trousers and a white shirt with frilled placket and cuffs. On his feet he wore ornately beaded moccasins, and upon his head was a cap that was military in style but made of rich black velvet decorated with quills and silk tassels, with a beaded band around it worked in a colorful geometric design. Physically he was not impressive—dark complexion, stocky build, and lustrous black hair that showed beneath his cap—but flanking the slightly hooked nose were the most intense eyes Ben had ever seen, and there was an aura of power about him.

The four who were approaching stopped a few feet from the raised area, and the man pointed at Ben and beckoned him forward, at the same time indicating that Little Buffalo and his parents should sit where they were, which they did. Ben, with trepidation rising in him, stepped up on the raised area and stopped a few feet in front of the man, who looked down at him for a long moment before the corners of his mouth twitched upward in a slight smile.

He made a vague gesture toward Little Buffalo's father and said in perfect English, "Walking Moose has told me you are called Ben and of how, the other day, you actually had the fearful *quiquihatch* eating out of your hand. He also told me of how you came to be here. But he knows of it only from the time when his son, Little Buffalo, plucked you off the surface of the mother water, Winnipeg, before she could devour you. I would hear from you who you are and where you live and how you came to be where Little Buffalo found you."

"Who . . . who are you, sir?" Ben asked, then flushed at the boldness of his question, but he did not drop his gaze as he added another: "How come you speak English?"

The man laughed with genuine amusement, and a concert of echoing laughter rippled briefly among those assembled, but stilled as the man continued. "You do not frighten easily. That is good. As for me, I am Louis Riel, but since I am named the same as my father, my people"—he swept out an arm to take in the onlookers—"call me David. Now, answer my questions. Little Buffalo says your name is Ben, but that is only your first name. What is your last name? Who are your parents, and where do they live? And how did you come to be adrift on the big water?"

"My last name," Ben replied, "is MacDonald. I'm Ben MacDonald, and my father and mother are William and Esther MacDonald. Our home is at Hawk's Hill. I was—"

Riel interrupted to say that he was not familiar with any place of that name, then, as Ben accurately described the location, the light of recognition dawned in the man's eyes.

"Ah," he said, nodding, "now I know where you mean. I have seen that farm from a distance several times but did not know who lived there or that it was called Hawk's Hill. So, now you must answer my last question: How did you happen to be where Little Buffalo found you?"

Haltingly at first, but then with increasing confidence, Ben related how, near his home at Hawk's Hill, he was attempting to escape from the big trapper he feared and who, he was convinced, was pursuing him; how he untied the boat and jumped in before he realized that the oars were not in the bottom as they should have been; how he had drifted down the Red River the rest of that day and all through the night and finally out into the lake, where he was rescued by Little Buffalo.

As the boy spoke, Riel held up his hand at intervals for him to pause and then skillfully interpreted into the Cree language for the intently listening assemblage what Ben had said, before motioning him to continue. When Ben concluded his account, Riel stood quietly for a short while, right elbow cradled in his left hand and right hand cupping his chin. His brows drew together in a faint frown, and he looked unseeingly for a time toward a dim corner of the big room. No one moved or spoke. At length he dropped his hands and again looked at Ben intently.

"Why do you think this man you call the trapper was after you in the first place?"

Ben's answer this time took much longer, for he had to back up to the events of more than a year ago to explain. He related an abbreviated version of the whole story, including how his lightly wounded father had driven the trapper away and how they had thought he was gone for good until he suddenly showed up at Hawk's Hill, causing Ben to flee from him and drift down the Red River in the oarless boat, over the rapids, and all the way out onto the expanse of Lake Winnipeg.

"It was all very scary," he admitted, concluding his narration, "and now I'm awful worried about my mother and father, because they don't know where I am or what happened to me. They may think Mr. Burton caught me and took me away. They may even think I'm dead!"

Louis Riel abruptly raised his hand, causing Ben to fall silent.

"Excuse me," the Metis leader said. He looked away from the boy, his gaze moving across the assemblage and then settling on two husky young men sitting together, and he beckoned them forward. He spoke to them without pause for several minutes and then the pair nodded and left the council house rapidly. Riel returned his attention to Ben.

"You have been gone from your home for a week today," he said, "and your parents must be very worried. I'm sorry I was away from here until yesterday, or I would have seen to this sooner. Even though very serious problems exist between your people and mine, I have sent Otter and Hunting Eagle to go to Hawk's Hill at once. They will approach under a white flag and let your parents know that you are safely with us and that I, personally, will be returning you to them in two days, as soon as I finish some business I must attend to here with my people."

A wave of mingled joy and relief surged through Ben, and he smiled broadly. For the first time since his arrival among the Metis, he now felt he was no longer in danger. He listened carefully as Riel went on.

"Hunting Eagle and Otter are good men," he said. "They will canoe upriver as fast as they can and should reach Hawk's Hill before sunset. Hunting Eagle has no English, but Otter can speak and understand enough of the language to give my message to your parents. It is important that your family know as soon as possible of your safety. If the trip upriver were not so dangerous, I would send you with them, but we cannot risk that. Besides, it would give me pleasure to return you to your parents myself, and I have instructed Otter to tell them this."

He paused for a brief span and then returned to

what Ben had been relating. "So, tell us, what of the *mistanask*—the badger. She survived being shot, did she?"

Ben's joy diminished, and his eyes filled with tears as he shook his head. "No, sir. She only lived through the night and then died, and we took her back out to her den and buried her in it." He sniffled and wiped his nose on his sleeve.

"Ah, that is too bad," Riel said gently. He rubbed an earlobe as he translated this last exchange, and the listeners stirred and murmured among themselves. They felt something very special had come upon them but did not know precisely what. The murmur silenced instantly as Riel dropped his hand, and when he spoke again, his voice had hardened.

"This trapper. Do you know his name?"

"It's Mr. Burton. George Burton."

Riel nodded. "I have seen this man several times, and I have spoken to him on two occasions, but that was a few years ago and I do not know him well. What little experience I have had with him, and what I know *of* him from what others have told me, even apart from what you have just told us, Ben, does not encourage me to become better acquainted with him."

He stopped speaking in English and addressed the assemblage in the Cree tongue, imparting to them this latest piece of information. Immediately there was a rising, unpleasant murmuring of voices. Riel listened to them for a few minutes, his expression darkening. Clearly, many of those present knew and disliked the big trapper even more than did their leader. When he half-raised his hand, however, the murmuring again died away and he turned back to the little boy.

"Many of my people know this man, and though they have traded with him for many years, they do not like or trust him. We first knew him here as a man who worked for the Hudson's Bay Company, but then he became a trapper and trader who worked only for himself. Time and again he has cheated my people in one way or another — selling some of them faulty goods, selling others damaged gunpowder that is mostly useless and cheap knives that will not hold an edge. He has sold us poorly made farming tools that quickly break under use, and he also sells at full price, to some of our people who crave alcohol, liquor to which he has secretly added an equal amount of water. He is allowed to trade among us only because he is one of the few who come here to provide us with goods we cannot otherwise get without making long and difficult journeys. He is said to be a dangerous man, cruel to Indians and animals alike when they are defenseless before him. He is a cowardly man, without honor or courage."

He paused for a long moment, as if it were only by great effort that he was able to dislodge the topic of Burton from his mind and return to the matter at hand. When he spoke again, his voice was brisk and light once more and he smiled at Ben.

"You have told us much, and I have told you only a little. I will tell you more about us, and about me, if you like, but what I have to say to you these others here already know. So now I will take you to my house and we will talk together."

Riel then spoke to those assembled crisply, briefly, in the Cree language, and at once they came to their feet and began streaming outside. In a few minutes the big chamber was empty save for Riel, Little Buffalo, his parents, and Ben. Riel spoke rapidly to the three Metis, and in a moment Walking Moose and Blue Flower Opening smiled and left as well.

"They will go home and await you there," Riel explained. "Little Buffalo will come with us. He will not be able to understand what we say, but there may be things that will come up in our talking that he should know, and I will tell him of these, and he will then be able to tell his father and mother. And he will escort you back to my house tomorrow morning, so I can tell you whatever news of your father and mother that Otter and Hunting Eagle have learned. Come."

He turned toward the open entry, and the two boys fell in side by side behind him. Outside, a portion of the people were still loosely gathered, their attention now focused on something that was occurring at one side of the central clearing. Riel immediately headed that way, Little Buffalo and Ben continuing to follow. The scattered people made way for them, and they soon could see what was causing the attraction. They stopped and watched, the boys flanking Riel.

Two large male dogs, one brindled, the other black, were fighting viciously, clinching in a wild tangle of flying fur, scuffling legs, and savagely snapping, lathering jaws. They broke apart and stiff-leggedly began circling each other, heads low to the ground, hackles raised to their limit, ears flattened against their skulls, and fierce snarls issuing from their mouths. Both were bleeding, the black one from a ripped ear and deeply gouged shoulder, the brindled one from a cheek torn open just below the eye.

"It is a fight to the death," Riel murmured to Ben.

"But . . . they're *hurting* each other!" Ben replied. "We've got to stop it." He started moving toward the savagely fighting dogs, but Riel instantly put out a hand and stayed him.

"No!" he said sharply. "It cannot be stopped now. They will attack anyone who tries to interfere, and then still they will fight until one of them is dead." He dropped his hand and shrugged, adding philosophically, "It is their way."

As Riel turned to repeat to Little Buffalo in Cree what he had said to Ben, the two large dogs continued to lunge and bite each other in deadly struggle. The snarlings and brief shrieks of pain became even louder, and Ben shook his head, dismayed at the injuries they were inflicting upon each other.

"That's terrible!" Ben protested. "I can't let them do that to each other. I *can't!*"

Before he could be prevented from doing so, Ben broke away from the onlookers, took several steps closer to the combatants, and then dropped to all fours and began crawling toward them. From his own throat came a strange combination of crooning, chattering, whining sounds, the same primal sounds he made during Burton's first visit to Hawk's Hill, when the trapper's dog, Lobo, had snarled at him and seemed sure to attack, until the dog had incomprehensibly grown calm and then even friendly.

There was a universal gasping and cries of concern from the onlookers, but Ben ignored them, his entire attention on the four-legged combatants, now only a few feet away. The watching Metis, including Riel and Little Buffalo, were too stunned to intervene, nor were they inclined to do so. This was something beyond their ken, something that demanded they only observe and not interfere.

Ben moved slowly but directly on hands and knees to the two bloody animals until he was close enough to reach them. The dogs became aware of him then and broke apart, still snarling in deadly earnest at each other. Ben continued making his strange sounds, and then, to the horror of the many onlookers, he reached out while still kneeling and touched the head of the black dog with his left hand and then the other one's head with his right. He neither petted them nor rubbed their ears, merely touched them, simultaneously increasing the volume of the strange crooning, whining, chattering sound. Almost visibly the insane rage consuming the animals seemed to drain away. For an unforgettable moment the scene became a frozen tableau, and then the brindled dog backed away a few steps, turned, and trotted off, limping slightly. The black dog remained a moment longer before turning his head and giving Ben's hand a single lick with his bloody tongue before loping off in the opposite direction.

The effect on the Metis was profound. They did not cheer or applaud or even speak, but they looked with awe at the little boy coming slowly to his feet, and in their own minds, they attributed what they had just witnessed to wonderful mystical powers. It was Louis Riel who put into words what all were thinking. In the Cree tongue he spoke softly, as much to himself as to the Indian lad beside him.

"When first I heard of what had happened with the *quiquihatch,* I found it hard to believe. Now I no longer have any doubts. The little one who has come among us is undoubtedly a great favorite of Kisemanitou."

CHAPTER 6

In the interval following his calming and separating the two savage dogs bent on killing each other, Ben MacDonald became even more of a celebrity among the Metis. News of his feat, which had been witnessed by so many, spread quickly, and within hours there was not a person in any of these five Metis villages who had not heard of it. The people who had been on hand to see it told the story over and over to those who hadn't, and those latter individuals bemoaned their ill fortune at having missed such an event. All believed Ben to be the vessel for a powerful spirit, and they regarded him with an awe that was now approaching reverence.

Even Louis Riel, who had been raised a Catholic and trained for the priesthood in Montreal under the guidance of Bishop Alexander Tache, remained convinced that there was something spiritually gifted about this little white boy. How else to explain that the child had lived practically a whole summer with so fierce a creature as a wild badger, engaging in cooperative acts with that animal that were beyond normal explanation? And what about the virtual miracle of his floating in a bulky, uncontrollable rowboat through the treacherous Red River rapids unscathed, which an adult male Metis in a highly maneuverable canoe would have hesitated attempting? And then, to top all else, there was the incredible incident with the *quiquihatch,* which was even more amazing than his separating the fighting dogs.

But while many came to see this little wonder named Ben, few got the opportunity to do so today, the reason being that after the council and dog fight, Ben and Little Buffalo spent many hours in quiet discussion with Riel in his private quarters. The leader's lodge was similar in construction to that in which Ben had been staying with Little Buffalo's family, but slightly bigger and divided inside into three rooms. In the principal room was a table and some chairs to sit on instead of buffalo-skin mats or woven reeds. It was one of the few structures in the village that had window openings, but there was no glass in them. Instead, they were covered with a material that allowed light to illuminate the interior nicely, yet which effectively blocked cold air from entering. Riel told him that the material was made by sewing together rabbit skins from which the hair had been removed and stretching them on frames until they were dry. Then bear oil was rubbed into them, and this caused the thin skins to lose their opacity and become translucent.

On the walls of this main room hung two guns, one very old and the other a modern rifle, both with leather cases hanging beside them. Also on the wall there were two bows, three quivers filled with arrows, and several spears and knives. The gun cases, as well as the quivers and the sheaths for the knives, were beautifully decorated with beadwork and quills, and the spears were painted and festooned with colorful ribbons.

Riel invited Ben and Little Buffalo to sit at the table with him, and there they talked together at considerable length. As much as Riel had previously discovered about him, it was now Ben who learned much about Riel and his people.

"We Crees have lived here for more than a thousand years," Riel began. "But since our villages are not located near the roads that the white men feel they must build through any new country they enter, few white people apart from occasional traders have ever come here, and those only in the past hundred years or so. There was only one major exception, which none of us living today witnessed, but which has been related to us through the generations by our tribal historians. A thousand summers ago, many white men—some with fiery red hair, others with hair the color of the autumn grasses—came among us in two huge canoes with tall carved images of strange, fiercely toothed animals in the front.

"When they were in the open waters far from land, they opened great sails and let the wind carry them, but when they came up the great river from Hudson Bay to the far north end of this lake"—he raised his hand in the direction of Lake Winnipeg—"dozens of men pulled in unison on long oars and defeated the strong river currents. When they reached the lake itself, they stopped rowing, and their sails carried them to us. They were friendly, and so we returned that friendship and welcomed them to stay among us. These were the strange white-skinned people who brought us the first metal tools and weapons we had ever seen."

Riel paused, remembering how he had sat and listened to the tribal historians tell of this momentous occurrence of the far distant past. In a moment he caught himself and continued. "They stayed with us for a long time, and while they were here, they sent out many parties of men to explore this whole region. Here and there they made strange marks on rocks, and in a few places—including even the place you call Hawk's Hill—they are said to have buried stores of weapons and tools and other things that would be of use to them when they came back again, as they planned to do. They even tried to ascend the Red River in their big boats, but damaged one of them at the first rapids and could not pass the second. When they returned here, they repaired the damage, and then they left us in the direction from which they had come, promising to return one day." He shook his head and added, "But they never came back again."

As he paused to pack some *osier*—crushed dry red willow leaves mixed with tobacco—into the bowl of a long-stemmed pipe, Ben took the opportunity to speak up.

"My teacher in school told us there were stories about white men—she called them Vikings—who came across the ocean hundreds and hundreds of years ago and, as they explored, finally came here. But she said most people think those are just made-up stories and didn't really happen."

As Ben spoke, Riel used some small metal tongs to lift a glowing coal from the fireplace and touch it to the tobacco in his pipe bowl, raising an eyebrow as Ben finished.

"Yes," he said, sucking on the pipe stem and blowing out a small cloud of fragrant smoke, "that is what they are called. Many do not believe they ever came here, but our tribal historians teach us—and I believe—that those stories are true. I have seen for myself the strange marks they have left on certain rocks."

He blew out another puff of smoke and then passed the pipe to Little Buffalo as he swiftly interpreted for him what he and Ben had been discussing. Little Buffalo puffed on the pipe briefly as their host had done and, in turn, passed it on to Ben. The little boy tried to emulate them but went into a spasm of coughing as soon as he sucked in a little smoke. Riel and Little Buffalo laughed, and Riel ruffled Ben's hair and said, "That's all right. I don't think you're quite ready for pipe smoking yet. Perhaps when you're a little older."

"I don't think so," Ben said, shaking his head and making a face at the bad taste the smoke had left in his mouth. "My father smokes a pipe, too, but I don't think I could ever get to like it." After a brief pause he asked, "What about you, Mr. Riel? Is this where you were born? And how did you happen to learn English and French?"

"No," the Metis leader replied, "I wasn't born here—that is, not right here in this village. I was born in 1844 in a small village on the Seine River, only a little over a mile from where it enters the Red near Fort Garry. There's a new village there now, a white man's town called St. Boniface. I had ten brothers and sisters, but I was the oldest. It was when I was fourteen that Bishop Tache sent me off to the seminary in Montreal because he thought I was an exceptional student and should study for the priesthood." He shrugged. "I learned a lot—French, which of course I knew, but I had to study it more, and also English, Greek, philosophy, and religion. But however much I learned, I didn't like being there, any more than they liked having me there. My teachers said I was quick-tempered, and I suppose that's true. Anyway, just before I was to be ordained as a priest, I quit. Just walked away. What I wanted was to be more like my father. He was a miller by trade and owned a gristmill, but he was also active in trade and soon discovered that most of the trading practices of the time were unfair to the Indians. He believed that all trade should be free and just, which it wasn't under the Hudson's Bay Company's control. And so he organized resistance to it, and in 1839, five years before I was born, he broke their monopoly."

Riel talked on, remembering his youth and early

manhood, the traveling he had done and the various jobs he had held in such places as Montreal, Chicago, and St. Paul. But somehow, he said, he had always come back to the Red River area, which was his home, among his people, the Metis.

"Things changed, though," he recalled. "We Metis have a proud heritage, both among the Crees and the French, though we are inclined toward the Cree culture. But we were being treated badly, discriminated against and called Half-Breeds, even in the official documents."

"My father," Ben interjected, "calls . . ." He broke off, suddenly embarrassed at what he had almost said.

"Go on," Riel encouraged him. "Your father calls what?"

"Well, he . . . he . . ." Ben's embarrassment grew, and he finished reluctantly, "He calls your people Half-Breeds." For the first time ever, Ben felt a twinge of shame for his father and was sorry he had responded to Riel's comment.

The Metis leader, however, took no offense. "A great many white people do," he murmured. After a slight pause he continued, "I have to admit I really became angry when I learned that the Hudson's Bay Company was actually trying to sell our land to the Dominion of Canada without even consulting us. And just as my father had opposed that company, so, too, did I."

"Well, weren't you afraid someone would try to hurt you?" Ben asked. "Maybe even try to kill you?"

Riel smiled. "Weren't you," he countered, "afraid the *quiquihatch*—or the dogs—would try to hurt you . . . maybe even kill you?" He shook his head faintly. "Ben, whether you can put it into words or not, I think you already know the answer. When you believe in something strongly enough, when you believe in your heart that what you are doing—or plan to do—is right, then you will do it, or fight for it, regardless of risks. And that's why my cousin and I did what we did."

Then he went on to explain how, only three years ago, in 1868, a team of surveyors led by Colonel J. S. Dennis came out from the Canadian capital to the Red River valley with orders to lay out Metis lands into plots, and that was before any kind of transaction had been made with those whose land it was—the Crees and the Metis. "To make matters even worse," Riel said, scowling, "they not only couldn't speak the Cree tongue, but they didn't even know French! The contempt with which they treated us was intolerable. My cousin, Andre Nault, and I gathered up sixteen other Metis warriors, and we confronted these intruders. We told them in both French and English that they must leave at once or suffer the consequences. Fortunately for them"—he smiled—"they left. But that didn't end it. In fact, that was only the beginning of this present trouble that your people are calling the Red River Rebellion."

He slammed his palm on the table and uttered an angry growl. When he resumed his account, it was almost as if he had forgotten Ben was there, and he spoke as if he were rallying his people. "Rebellion? Rebellion against whom? We are not *subjects*. We owe allegiance to no one but ourselves — our culture, our people, our heritage. But they wouldn't listen to us. The Canadian government went ahead and illegally bought our lands from the Hudson's Bay Company and then turned right around and gave them to settlers and farmers, so they could come in and cut down our forests, burn our prairies, and plant vegetable gardens over the graves of our fathers."

Ben knew his own father was one of those farmers Riel was referring to, and he immediately came to his defense. "My father says the land was just going to waste. He says the Half- . . . the Metis didn't plant much of anything and you weren't using it anyway."

Riel shook his head, expressionless but seeming more agitated at the remark than he allowed himself to show outwardly. He responded more with sadness than anger. "Of course we used it, but mostly for hunting. You don't destroy the fields and forests the animals depend on if you want them to stay and increase

111

in numbers. But that's not the point. Even if we didn't use it at all, it's *still* our land, and that doesn't give others the right to come in and take it away from us."

He made a brief sound, half-groan, half-growl, and continued with his narration, leaning over the table toward Ben.

"Many of our younger men, who had difficulty controlling their tempers, wanted to attack the people who were encroaching on these lands and drive them away or kill them, but our leaders discussed this, and we knew it would not solve our problems to harm those settlers and farmers; they weren't the enemy. It was the government that was doing this, and we had to get *its* attention."

Riel abruptly checked his rising fervor and sat back in his chair. "The Metis looked to me for leadership and asked me what could be done. I considered this carefully and decided there was only one way. The Canadian government had declared that they would not negotiate with us as a tribal people; they would negotiate only with another government. It was clear to me that this was what we had to become. So, a year ago last November, I led a force of our warriors to Fort Garry. We seized the place and set up a provisional government, and that was what at last forced the Canadian government to negotiate directly with us. And that," he said, a measure of pride in his voice, "is what resulted in the admission of Manitoba as a province last July."

"When I was living in the den with the badger," Ben said.

"Yes, exactly at that time," Riel agreed. "We thought that would end our problems and we would be left in peace, but unfortunately, little has changed. Manitoba is now a province, true, with a voice in Canadian government, but we Metis, who caused this to happen, are still treated with contempt, and we are still referred to as Half-Breeds by the whites who have now come back to control Manitoba's provincial government. And so our struggle for justice and equality continues, and that struggle is still being called the Red River Rebellion today."

While Ben did not fully grasp all the complexities of the events Riel was relating, he was fascinated by the man and amazed that the Metis leader would talk with him like this, as if he were an adult rather than just a boy. That was something rare in his young life, and he felt honored and pleased.

It appeared that Riel had more to say, but just then a babble of excited voices arose from outside, and a moment later the heavy buffalo skin — *paskwawi-mustusweyan*—cloaking the doorway was thrust aside. A large man stood there, awaiting an invitation to enter. Riel, smiling, leaped to his feet and went to him.

He clapped him on both shoulders and then wrapped him in a great hug. Little Buffalo, who had been sitting quietly all this time, unable to follow the conversation, now wore a pleasantly surprised expression.

The two men at the doorway held a brief animated conversation in a mixture of French and Cree. Then Riel indicated Ben, and the stranger stepped in and stopped close to the boy. Appearing to be older than Riel by some eight or ten years, the man was both taller and more muscular. His garb was roughly similar to Riel's, except that slung over one shoulder he carried a rifle in a lavishly bead-ornamented case.

The man studied Ben's appearance. When their eyes locked, the boy held the gaze without falter. The man smiled and placed a hand on Ben's shoulder. His voice, when he spoke, was deeper, with more of a rumbling, resonant quality than Riel's.

"*Ekwa, eoko ka wanisik napesis mamiywe ka kaskittat kita mikwasiwatat pikwatchi pisiskiwa. Wasaskuteya-piw.*" He chuckled and ruffled Ben's hair, adding, "*Ni ka sakihaw awah, nit'iteyitten.*" His gaze switched to the Metis boy, and he made another comment Ben couldn't understand.

He turned then and strode out, murmuring a comment to Riel and touching his arm as he passed. Riel was smiling as he returned to the boys and took his seat again. He addressed Ben.

"That was a good friend of mine, Ben. He seems to have been impressed by you."

"Who is he?" Ben asked. "What did he say while he was looking at me?"

"He had heard about you from the others outside, and he said, 'So this is the little lost boy who can smooth away the fury of savage animals with no more than a touch.' Then he said you have eyes that are clear and strong and that he thought he could grow to like you. And he told Little Buffalo that he did well and that his father could be proud of him. Everything he said is quite true. As for who he is, he is our greatest warrior, our military general. He is also my dearest friend. His name is Gabriel Dumont.

"Perhaps one day, if there is time for us, I will tell you a great deal about him, but for now I will tell you only a little and then I must leave and talk privately with him. He was born close to here seven years before me. When he was only two summers old, his father moved their family far to the southeast, in what is now the United States, to a place where two large rivers join to form an even greater river called the Ohio. There, his father worked at Fort Pitt as a trader. When Gabriel was eleven, they returned to this area, and by then he could speak six different Indian languages perfectly, as well as French. Unfortunately he has no English. Did you see the rifle he had with him?"

"I saw part of it sticking out of its cover. There was an awful lot of fancy beadwork on that cover."

"It's a very special case for a very special gun that he named *Le Petit*. It was his first gun, given to him when he was only eleven to honor him for an act of bravery during that trip from Fort Pitt back to the Red River. He always has it with him and takes excellent care of it. It was the gun he used in his first major conflict, when he was fourteen and took part in the Battle of Coteau against the Dakota Sioux, against whom we were then at war. When the war ended, he became a trapper and fisher in this area, and he and one of your people, Dunblane, built a ferry across the Red River. But more than anything else he is a great warrior and strategist."

Riel shoved his chair back and stood up. "And now I must go," he said. "We will talk again tomorrow morning, and on the following day I will take you home. In the meanwhile, Little Buffalo will continue to take care of you."

Riel then turned to Little Buffalo and spoke to him rapidly in Cree. Once or twice the Metis boy replied to a question, but mostly he just listened and nodded. When Riel finished, he patted the youth on the shoulder and then pulled aside the *paskwawi-mustusweyan* over the doorway and left.

Ben was curious about what the Metis leader had

said to Little Buffalo, but his ability in the Cree language was still much too rudimentary for him to successfully question the older boy about it, so he simply waited. When Little Buffalo turned to him and indicated through sign language that they should leave now, he nodded and followed him outside.

They made their way through the milling people, who now pressed forward to catch a glimpse of the magical little white boy. They parted to let the boys go by, many of them saying things to Ben that he could not understand, others reaching out to touch him for just an instant as he passed. The pair left the village and walked back to Walking Moose's lodge in Maskwa, and for the rest of the day Little Buffalo tried to explain to him, with occasional Cree words but more often through sign language and sketchy pictures he drew in the soil with a stick, various things about the village and the people who lived in it.

Ben was particularly fascinated by a game two groups of boys were playing with a wad of feathers tied into a ball. Each boy had a stout stick on the end of which was a small triangular framework with narrow strips of rawhide woven into a shallow basket. The object seemed to be for each group of boys to get deep into the territory of the opposing group by any means possible, and toss the feathered ball into a circle on the ground that was made of wrapped willow withes. The group without possession of the feathered ball tried to keep this from happening, again by almost any means possible. It was a rough game, with a lot of kicking and shoving and often with heads being thumped or noses bloodied with the sticks, but the boys seemed to take the knocks and minor injuries in stride and cheered lustily whenever the goal was successfully accomplished. Little Buffalo called the game *lacrosse*.

The more he saw, the more Ben was intrigued by the ways of the Metis. And, even though he was worried about his own family and wanted to be back with them, another part of him wished he could spend a long time here to learn much more. He decided that, assuming he would get back home again before very long, he would someday come back here for an extended visit that would allow him to learn their language and much more about their whole way of life.

Having some time ago eaten his fill with Little Buffalo's family, he lay in the darkness of their little lodge and thought about the many things Louis Riel had told him. He could not help admiring the leader, and he found himself feeling sorry for the Metis, who had shown him nothing but kindness. He also found himself wondering why his mother distrusted these people and why his father feared them and called them Half-Breeds. He was confused and wondered why some people said hurtful things about other people.

He remained excited and gratified over the prospect of finally being taken home the day after tomorrow by Louis Riel, but the buoyant feeling suddenly drained away when a new—and very frightening—possibility occurred to him. Up to now he had worried about George Burton catching him and what would happen if that occurred. Now, however, he was chagrined at having thought only of himself. What if the big trapper decided to seek revenge against his parents, against his brother and sisters? The man was dangerous and unpredictable, and the entire MacDonald family, not just Ben himself, could be in jeopardy.

Try as he might, Ben could not shake off this new fear.

CHAPTER  7

Esther MacDonald was having a difficult time maintaining her composure and had thus far managed to do so only because she knew that if she let loose the emotions seething within her, it could not help but affect the girls similarly, perhaps even more. Beth and Coral were frightened and disconsolate enough as it was, not only over Ben's disappearance but because now their father and older brother were overdue and all sorts of terrible imaginings were running through their minds.

Though they hadn't admitted it, at least not to her, Esther was sure that both her daughters believed that Ben was dead. They were also terrified over the possibility that had eventually occurred to them, that George Burton might return while their father and older brother were gone. The realization brought on nightmare thoughts about what would happen then. Their mother's declaration that she would shoot him if he did show up did little to ease their fear.

This was the third morning since William and John had ridden off in search of Ben and the boat, and her husband had clearly indicated that he expected to be back, at the latest, by late afternoon yesterday. It was also the sixth morning since Ben's disappearance, and unlike the several neighbors who had stopped by to pay their respects because of their mounting conviction that the little boy was dead, Esther had grown ever more convinced not only that Ben was still alive but that he needed help badly.

She was no less concerned for William and John, but they were grown men — well, almost, in the case of John — and could fend for themselves. Ben, on the other hand, was so . . . so *little*. So defenseless. Somehow she had to find him, help him. And as certain as she was that Ben was still alive, so was she equally certain that he had been captured by the Metis Indians and taken to their villages on the other side of the Red River.

Esther's intolerance of the Metis had never been quite so pronounced as her husband's, but she did tend to distrust them, and she was more than just a little afraid of them. Nevertheless, her determination to help Ben overshadowed that fear, and she knew what she had to do. She simply could not bear the thought of another day of inactivity, another day of just being here with the girls and doing nothing but waiting.

Early this morning, well before dawn, she had awakened and lay there in bed thinking of just these things, and she had come to a decision: She would go to the Metis herself to learn if they had her little son. If, in fact, Ben was with them, she would convince them to return him safely to her. Exactly how she would do this she was not entirely sure, but, as she muttered to herself in the lingering darkness, "I've always been able to do just about anything I set my mind to do, and, with the help of God, I can do this. I know I can. And I will!"

She had quietly slipped out of bed and gathered up what few items she would need, such as jerky and a packet of cornmeal, plus a few things that might be useful in dealing with the Indians—spools of brightly colored silk thread, needles, scissors, even a small hand mirror—and put them in a pouch. Then she woke the girls and told them to get up, get dressed, pack some extra clothing into a bag, and come downstairs. Where normally they would have complained or demanded answers to the questions that bubbled inside them, her uncustomary brusqueness subdued them, and they did as she bade, silently and not a little fearfully.

Esther had a breakfast of bacon and scrambled eggs already on the kitchen table when they came down. Even though the very thought of food was repugnant to her this morning, Esther ate with them, knowing that she would need the sustenance for what lay ahead. God only knew when—or where, for that matter—she would eat a hot meal again. They spoke sparingly to each other as they ate, and the distress of the girls over their mother's preoccupied state of mind increased considerably when Esther dropped her fork with a clatter onto her plate and stood up.

"I have something to do," she said, "but I'll be back in a few minutes. You girls do the dishes while I'm gone."

Without waiting for a response, she tossed a light shawl over her shoulders, opened the kitchen door, and stepped outside. It was becoming daylight now, though the sun had not yet risen, and she went directly to the barn, where she hitched her little mare, Pirouette, to the buggy and secured her saddle, its blanket, and her pouch to the luggage carrier behind. She then led Pirouette to the house, tied her at the rail, and went back inside, her mood having lightened measurably now that she was actually doing something she felt was worthwhile. She found the girls had finished with the dishes and were sitting silently on opposite ends of the divan.

"I'm sorry I've been short with you this morning," she apologized. "I had a bad night. Just stay there and I'll be with you in a minute."

Esther returned to the kitchen, found a piece of paper and a pencil in a drawer, and swiftly wrote out a note. She weighted it down on the kitchen table with a heavy pewter spoon, made a quick check to be certain all the lanterns were out, then returned to the parlor.

"Let's go, girls. I'll tell you where we're heading as soon as we're on the move."

They left the house, and the girls climbed up into the buggy, tossed their bag into the back seat, and settled themselves on the bench seat in front while their mother untied Pirouette and then joined them. For an instant Esther considered taking along one of the guns but decided against it. She chirped and snapped the reins, turning the little mare and immediately sending her into a trot, following the road south.

Just over half an hour later and some six miles from Hawk's Hill, Esther reined Pirouette off the main road into the lane leading a quarter-mile to the big old farmhouse that was the home to the MacCombers, their nearest neighbors. The older couple came out onto the veranda as the buggy came to a stop at their hitching rail in front of the house.

"Mary, Dan," Esther greeted them, "I need a favor. Can you take care of Beth and Coral till I come back? I don't know how long I'll be gone. Maybe a couple of days. Maybe even more. I just don't know."

"Of course we'll take care of them, Esther," Mary replied, concern etched in her expression and evident in her voice, "but where are you going?"

Esther motioned to the girls, who hugged and kissed her in turn, retrieved their clothing bag, and clambered out. They were subdued, and their eyes were reddened. Esther got out, too, shaking her head as she went to the rear of the buggy.

"I haven't the time to explain everything right now," she said, freeing the saddle, blanket, and pouch and draping them over the hitching rail. "It's rather involved." She continued talking as she unhitched Pirouette from the rig and saddled her. Aware of Dan's painful lumbago, she waved away his move to help her. "Thanks, Dan—I've got it. Now, then, I've told the girls everything, and they'll explain it to you. It's not likely, but if William and John should stop by here, just tell them what Coral and Beth will be telling you and urge them to follow me as quickly as they can." Finished cinching the girth, she firmly tied the cord of her pouch over the horn, slipped a foot into the stirrup, and smoothly lifted herself astride the saddle.

"Beth, Coral"—she turned to the girls—"you be good and do just as Mr. and Mrs. MacComber say." She felt a pang as she saw that they were both crying. "I love you, my dears, so very much. Don't worry—I'll be all right. And I'll be back soon." She blew them a kiss, tossed a quick wave at the neighbors, said, "Thanks," and then put Pirouette into a gallop back down the long lane.

At the main road, she turned south again and continued another two miles to the trail that led off eastward to Dunblane's place on the west shore of the Red River, hoping desperately that the bluff old Scotsman would be there.

Ten years ago, when there were no particular troubles prevailing with the Indians, Devlin Dunblane had, with great effort and with the assistance of the famed Metis warrior Gabriel Dumont, rigged a rope ferry across the river; it was operated by use of a hand winch and several pulleys. The ferryboat itself was hardly deserving of the name, since it was nothing more than a log-and-board raft large enough to carry two horses, some supplies, and two or three people in a single crossing. But Esther knew that in recent years, as problems with the Metis had increased,

Gabriel Dumont had withdrawn from association with the operation, and it was very difficult for Dunblane to work it alone. Using the makeshift winch he had constructed to pull the ferry across took both physical strength and considerable effort, and it was becoming too exhausting for him.

Then, too, Esther knew, with the death of his wife from consumption only a little over a year ago, Dunblane had lost much of his desire to do anything beyond drinking more than he should. She hoped that, in view of the urgency of her circumstances, he would make an exception in this case.

As she arrived at the little Dunblane cabin, her hopes were quickly dashed. Devlin Dunblane came unsteadily outside as she rode up, and he listened as she made her request, but he was shaking his grizzled head before she finished.

"Och, lassie," he said, " 'tis sorry I am indeed that I canna help ye. Two reasons, there are. First, I've been fighting a divil of a cold for a week, an' barely able to get around even now, y'know. Further," he went on regretfully, "the ropes've become too rotted and frayed to use the ferry anymore until I c'n replace 'em. Fact is, Miz MacDonald, I'm not even sure I *will* replace 'em. Been considering selling out to someone younger and with more drive than I've got these days."

Dismayed but undaunted, Esther looked down at

him, refusing to be thwarted. "Then I'll swim my horse across," she said.

"Och, lass, ye dinna want t'do that." He hooked a gnarled thumb toward the stream. "She's of a strong current out there, y'know, an' a long ways across. Ye're naught but a woman. T'would take a hearty mon an' a bigger an' stronger mount than ye've got here." He patted Piroutte's neck.

"You underestimate both me and my horse, Mr. Dunblane," she said grimly, reining sharply away from him. With no further delay, she thumped her heels into Pirouette's sides, forcing the mare forward and into the river.

While the Red River here was neither quite so swift nor so turbulent as where it passed Hawk's Hill, some eight miles below, it was a bit broader at this crossing place and still a formidable stream. Pirouette surged through the shallows and then, when her hooves no longer touched bottom, swam strongly to about the midpoint. Then she began to gasp and blow heavily, and her eyes bulged with her efforts to master the powerful current. They were swept downstream much more rapidly than they were making forward progress, and by the time they were three-fourths of the way across, Esther could see that Pirouette's strength was rapidly failing.

Taking a good grip on the saddle, Esther slid off the mare's back on the downstream side, easing the animal's load and even trying to help their progress by kicking her feet, in the process of which she lost both shoes and her shawl. The water was very cold, and she soon began numbing. Her hands suddenly slipped off the slick leather of the saddle, and she flailed in the water. One hand touched something, and she snatched it. It was Pirouette's tail. She gripped it desperately and then brought up the other hand and clutched the tail with that one as well. Buffeted and swirled, Pirouette continued to swim gallantly but weakly. And then, just as Esther was beginning to think they were lost, Pirouette's hooves touched bottom and she found her footing. With enormous effort and still dragging Esther behind, she staggered into the shallows and finally reached the shore. The bank here had a steep pitch, and at first the mare failed in her efforts to climb out. Finally she gave up trying and simply stood there, shivering and blowing heavily.

"Good girl, good girl," Esther said, moving up closer and grasping the bridle. She patted the mare's neck and kissed the soft muzzle. "I knew you could do it, Pirouette. Good girl."

A glance about disclosed a place where the bank was much less steep, and she led the weary mare there and coaxed her into another effort. Together they scrambled up through brush to more level ground. There was a faint trail here, and she walked her horse along it a dozen yards or so to a small glade where they could rest for a while. Here she looped Pirouette's reins around a low-hanging branch.

Esther's pouch was still attached to the saddle horn, and she was thankful that she had tied it firmly at the MacComber place. She took it down and checked the contents, which were wet but largely undamaged. The spools of thread were soaked through, but they would dry well enough. The packet of cornmeal was another matter. Both packet and meal were saturated, and she knew it would quickly spoil, so she stuffed a handful into her mouth and gave the remainder to Pirouette.

She was still shivering from her immersion and wished she had the means for building a fire to dry her clothes. Fortunately, the day was warming and the sun shone brightly into the little glade. She had not worn stockings and was barefoot now, which she realized could present some problems later, but there was no help for it. She removed her blouse and skirt, wrung the excess water out of them, and spread them out on the ground in the full sunlight. After a moment's hesitation she also removed her petticoat and chemise and did the same with them. Now unclothed except for her knickers, which covered her from the waist to just above the knees, she suddenly giggled, thinking that the last time she was in such a condition in such a place was when she and some of her schoolgirl chums, all in their mid-teens, had daringly gone skinny-dipping in a swimming hole. How long ago that was!

Still chuckling a little, Esther got a couple of sticks of jerky out of the pouch and sat down to munch on them, her back against the bole of a large cottonwood tree. The warmth of the sun felt good on her skin, and after eating the jerky, she felt a little sleepy, so she drew up her knees, folded her arms across them, and lay her head down. In moments she was asleep.

When she awoke, she was stiff and chilled. The glade was now partially in shade, including where she was sitting, but the drying clothes were still in full sunlight. Esther guessed she must have been dozing for an hour, perhaps more, and immediately regretted the loss of time. She swiftly donned her clothes, which were much drier than before, though still damp and clammy. Ignoring the discomfort, knowing they would dry as she rode toward the Metis villages, she re-tied the pouch to the saddle horn and was just on the verge of mounting Pirouette when she heard a sound behind her.

Startled, gripped with the instant fear of Indians, she whirled around. Her eyes widened and a sharp gasp caught in her throat, but not because it was a Metis who rode into the little glen.

It was the widely grinning, densely bearded trapper, George Burton.

CHAPTER 8

Some four hours after arriving home at Hawk's Hill, William and John MacDonald were once again mounted on their geldings and heading away, their concerns now substantially increased.

It had been just after sunrise on this seventh day of Ben's disappearance, that the father and son had topped a low rise and saw Hawk's Hill in the distance before them. Both were grateful beyond measure at the sight but, equally, so bone weary that their reactions had been subdued.

"Well, there's home," William said.

"Sure is," John agreed, adding, "at last."

At that moment it seemed to both of them that they

had been riding without pause for days. They hadn't been, of course, but with the exception of only a few brief stops to give the horses some rest, this particular stint of riding, since finally giving up their search near the abandoned rowboat, had consumed twenty-four hours—a very full day.

After awakening at dawn yesterday and eating the last of their rations, they once again checked out the boat, wedged in the fallen pine. They had to be sure there was no clue in it to Ben's whereabouts that they may have overlooked. Aside from the fish bag, which they had seen the evening before, there was nothing. Once more they carefully checked the branches of the tree and the shoreline beneath the overhanging slanted trunk, as well as the ground all around the uprooted base. Again, nothing. They had been disappointed, but at least they would not be haunted later by the thought that perhaps they had not made a thorough enough search.

The new sun had just appeared above the lake's surface when they mounted up and began the tedious ranging back and forth, each in his own ever-expanding arc. Their eyes strained to take in every twig, every blade of grass, every patch of exposed soil, no matter how small. By late forenoon, when they had been riding steadily for nearly six hours, they had reached the conclusion that there was no reasonable likelihood that Ben could have been in the boat when it had finally become wedged in the tree. Which, if he had not drowned, left only one logical conclusion: He was in the hands of the Metis.

"So now what, Papa?"

"I told your mother that I expected we'd be back by late afternoon today at the latest. Obviously we'll miss that mark by a great deal. She'll be very worried. The girls, too." William gave his son an appraising look. "How are you holding up, John? Can you handle a long hard ride?"

The youth grinned wryly. "How long is long? How hard is hard?"

"Straight home from here with no more camps. I figure about eighteen hours from now to get there. And then, after we rest, on to the Red River crossing and directly to that Half-Breed town we saw."

John breathed a silent whistle and then grinned again, this time with more humor. "Betcha I'll hold up better than you. Let's go."

So they had set out southward, every now and then zigzagging back and forth a few hundred yards on each side for perhaps a quarter-mile before resuming the straight southward ride. Twice they found human tracks: both times moccasined feet, one medium-size, the other large. Each time the elder MacDonald muttered the same epithet: "Half-Breed vermin!"

By mid-afternoon the horses were becoming jaded, occasionally stumbling. The homeward bound searchers stopped every couple of hours to give the animals a quarter-hour rest. It helped a little, but each pause became noticeably less effective than the one before. In addition to the pervading weariness, horses and riders alike were extremely hungry. Before sunset they gave up on the sporadic zigzagging maneuver and just plodded wearily straight onward.

Into the twilight. Into the darkness. Into the breaking of dawn.

And then, finally, they had crested the little rise and there was Hawk's Hill before them, bathed in the roseate gold of the sunrise. That last mile to the house had been the hardest, filled as it was with such overwhelming expectation—the anticipation of food, bath, rest, mother, wife, family, *home*.

William had thought it strange that no one came out to greet them as they neared the house, and a niggling of concern had risen in him. John, too, was experiencing the same thoughts.

"Papa," he had said, "you go right in. I'll see to the horses."

William nodded, handing his reins to John and stepping stiffly down from the saddle, wondering fleetingly as he did so how this boy had grown up so quickly, how he had become so responsible an individual.

As John plodded on toward the barn, leading his father's horse, William stepped up onto the veranda and entered the parlor. A house breathes with the lives of those within it, and there was no sense of that here. It was eerily quiet inside.

"Esther?" William called. "Esther!"

No response. He walked to the foot of the staircase and repeated the calls upward. Still nothing. Both shotgun and rifle were still hanging on their wall pegs. He went into the kitchen and immediately saw the note held down by the heavy cooking spoon. Relieved, he snatched it up and read the words in his wife's familiar script. His relief drained away as he did so.

Dearest William, John —

Where are you? Am haunted with worry over you. I am convinced Ben is alive and that the Indians have him. Can no longer just stay here waiting, doing nothing, so I'm heading out to find him. The girls will be staying with the MacCombers. I plan to cross the river at Dunblane's, then north to the Metis villages. Follow as soon as you can. I love you both.

Esther

William's immediate impulse had been to rush away after her, try to overtake her, keep her from heading into such jeopardy, but common sense prevailed, because to do that was insanity. They and the horses *had* to have food and rest. And so, the horses having been unsaddled and put into their stalls with abundant fresh grain and fodder, father and son also ate—thick slabs of ham fried with slices of potatoes, applesauce, Esther's good bread thickly smeared with strawberry jam.

They had agreed that three hours of sleep before taking up the pursuit would suffice—enough time to refresh them and the horses, to a degree at least. They collapsed on their beds, only kicking off their shoes, and John was almost instantly asleep. William, his mind awhirl with thoughts of Ben possibly captured by the Metis, of Esther possibly in danger, of concern for the girls and John, was sure he would not be able to sleep, despite how tired he was. He wondered how much of a head start Esther had on them and wished she had written what time—or even day—it was when she wrote the note . . . and in the midst of that thought he fell asleep.

Instead of three hours, nearly four had passed when William jerked in his sleep and then sat bolt upright, knowing immediately that he had slept longer than intended. Mentally berating himself while donning his shoes, he called loudly to John and got him moving. They tossed a new supply of jerky and chunks of bread into the packs, snatched up their rifles, and ran to the barn. The horses seemed remarkably rejuvenated, and William grudgingly admitted it had undoubtedly been good for them to have the extra hour's rest. They saddled up without delay.

Now, just a little over four hours from the time they had reached home, they were on the road again, heading south. Since Coral and Beth were safely ensconced with Dan and Mary, and the sense of urgency in them was great to possibly overtake Esther, who might well be in serious trouble, they passed the long lane leading to the MacComber place without turning in and rode directly to Dunblane's. The old Scot emerged from the cabin as they rode up.

"Ye dinna have to ask," he said, speaking before they had even come to a halt. "She was here. Maybe five, six hours ago."

"You took her across, Devlin?" William asked, reining in.

Dunblane grunted a negative sound. "Couldn't. 'Part from me ailing, the ferry's down. Ropes're all rotted an' frayed."

"Well, where'd she go, then?"

"Right where she aimed to. Across. Verra headstrong, she is." He chuckled.

William's exasperation was beginning to show. "For God's sake, Devlin, how'd she get across?"

"Why, swam that little mare of hers, a'course. Never thought she'd make it. Surely didn't." He shook his head.

"You didn't try to stop her?" William growled, and simultaneously John asked, "My mother got across all right?"

"An' how was I t'do that, MacDonald?" Dunblane answered the man. "Like I said, verra headstrong." His gaze shifted to John. "Oh, aye, laddie. She got across. Way downstream it t'were, an' fell off 'fore she got there. But that bonny little mare pulled 'er right out, she did." He pointed downstream. "See that biggest tree way down there t'other side? Came out just a mite below that."

The elder MacDonald and son looked at each other and knew what they had to do. Both their geldings were bigger and stronger than Esther's mare. John gave a fatalistic little shrug, and then the same wry smile touched his lips.

"Let's do it, Papa."

William nodded and glanced at the old man. "Thanks, Devlin."

He heeled his mount forward into the river, and John followed closely behind. The current swept them downstream even faster than they'd expected, but they made good headway at first. Less than halfway across, however, William's gelding began to falter badly. John tried to turn his mount and get it upstream of him to break the current a little, but the thrust of the water was too powerful and he was now twenty or thirty feet downstream from him and still slightly behind. His father's horse was struggling desperately and still moving closer to the other side, but the big gelding was swimming lower and lower in the water as exhaustion took its toll. When they were two-thirds of the way across, only the horse's head, tilted up sharply, was still out of water, and then it abruptly submerged and was gone.

William thrashed free, and the rifle slipped out of his hands and disappeared. Nearby his horse broke the surface again, struggling weakly, then submerged once again. This time it did not reappear. The current whirled William fiercely, thrusting him close to John, who was still clinging grimly to his mount with one hand. With the other hand, John clasped his own rifle by the barrel and extended it as far as he could. William's flailing hand touched it, and he grasped at the stock, seizing it desperately. Holding on, he was swung by the current to the side of the horse. With his free hand, he felt for and found the top of the cinch strap where it attached to the saddle, and he managed to get a good grip on it.

John's mount was now struggling, too, eyes and nostrils wide with fear, blowing and gasping. But just then the gelding found footing and surged into shallower water, dragging William along, who got his own feet back under control just as they reached the shore. The bank was not too steep here, and they made their way to the top safely. John dismounted and went to his father.

"Are you all right, Papa?"

Wheezing some from his exertions, William nodded. "I can't imagine how Esther made it across there with little Pirouette." He cupped the side of John's neck in his hand. "I wouldn't've made it without your help. I'm glad you're safe, son. But we lost a good horse. My gun, too."

John nodded, patting the neck of his own gelding, who had overcome the fright and was now beginning to nibble at some leaves on a small bush. "We'd better see if we can pick up Mama's trail."

They found they had come ashore not far from the big tree Devlin Dunblane had pointed out from the other side and, only ten yards below that, where Esther and Pirouette had come ashore. The mare's tracks led northward along a faint trail, and, John afoot and William riding, they followed them a short distance to the glen. There they found tracks showing that Pirouette had been tied for a while, as well as the remains of a sodden bag that still held the residue of cornmeal. They also found several small prints of bare feet.

"Looks like your mother may have lost her shoes," William said, squatting down to more closely examine the prints.

"Or maybe she just took them off to dry them," John suggested, ranging out a little farther as he studied the ground. Abruptly he stiffened. "Papa," he said, "someone else was here."

William moved over to him at once, and together they studied first the hoofprints of a different horse, obviously larger than Pirouette, then the deep print of a big moccasined foot. They followed to where there were indications of a struggle. Then the tracks of both horses continued northward on the trail.

William groaned and muttered his familiar remark again: "Filthy Half-Breed vermin! They got her."

John, looking closer, disagreed. "I don't think so. Those moccasin prints look different than the ones we saw yesterday. It's a big man. Look at the size of 'em, and how deep they are. And, Papa, the hoofprints— they're from a shod horse. The Metis don't have many horses, and they don't shoe the ones they have. These are from a white man's horse."

"But whose?" William said.

The father and son straightened then and looked at each other with an awful realization suddenly dawning in their eyes and, with it, a new rush of apprehension.

Burton.

CHAPTER 9

Esther MacDonald quickly realized the futility of struggling against the three sets of rawhide tugs that bound her. The more she pulled against the long thin strips of rawhide, the tighter they became.

One set of tugs bound her wrists together, allowing her limited control of Pirouette's reins. The second set, looped from one ankle to the other, kept her legs tight against her horse's flanks and were tied together beneath the mare's belly, effectively preventing any possibility of Esther leaping off and trying to run away. The final set was the worst — one end was snugged around her throat and the other end was tied to Pirouette's bridle, with precious little slack, which eliminated the possibility of her kneeing the mare into a gallop to escape, since the forward thrusting of the horse's head in a gallop could strangle her. George Burton was apparently well experienced in preventing captives from escaping.

Now, as they followed the narrow river trail northward toward the Metis villages at the mouth of the Red River, Esther looked at the huge man on the horse ahead of her, a ten-foot tether from her horse to his saddle. He hadn't looked back at her with that repulsive black-bearded face for many minutes now, and she was thankful for that, because the way he looked at her sent chills down her spine. She was infinitely grateful that the big man had not shown up in the glade when she was still asleep and largely unclothed.

She did not know what Burton had in mind to do with her, but she was frightened, having already experienced his brute strength. Her right cheek was sore and swollen from where he had struck her in their initial tussle, and her upper right arm was showing a large, spreading bruise through the torn sleeve of her blouse. There was also a deep painful throbbing pulsing through her whole left leg from the injured foot.

The horrible memory of that unexpected encounter with the big trapper was one she knew she would never be able to erase from her memory, no matter how hard she tried. Now, riding as they were at a steady walking gait, she once again relived in her mind how all this had come about, wondering if somehow she might have done something to avoid her present predicament.

When she had heard that noise behind her in the glen and spun around and saw George Burton, she reacted immediately, as did he. She had leaped away instantly even as he had lunged from his saddle at her. In her desperation, she sped away as fast as she could run, dodging the trees, outstretched branches, and dense brushy areas of this river valley growth. He was much bigger and stronger and certainly could run faster than she, but her smaller size and litheness allowed her to slip through narrow gaps that he had to either detour around or bull his way through.

She not only maintained the gap between them for a while but actually began widening it—until she encountered the storm-toppled remains of a pine tree in her path. The trunk was about three feet off the ground, and without breaking stride, she gathered up her flapping skirt and leaped high to clear it. She did so easily, by six or seven inches, but she did not see, until too late, the jagged broken stub of a branch as thick as her thumb projecting from the trunk. It plunged deeply into the sole of her foot, and the weight of her momentum snapped it off close to the trunk.

She screamed and fell to the ground, writhing in agony. She grasped the stub sticking out of her foot and tried to pull it out but nearly fainted from the pain, and then it was too late; Burton was upon her. She tried to squirm away, but his beefy hand closed on her upper right arm with such strength she thought the bone would break. She clawed at his eyes while wrenching out of his grasp, and a portion of her sleeve, from shoulder to elbow, came away in his hand. Her clawing fingers missed his eyes but gouged furrows in the flesh of his temple and across his cheekbone.

Burton snarled a vile profanity and jerked back, but she kicked at his face with her wounded foot. He was fast, and his hand flashed up to catch the foot but closed instead around the stub and unwittingly he did what she herself had been unable to do; he jerked it free of her foot with an oath and threw it aside. With a short chopping swing of the same hand, now balled into a fist, Burton struck her a meaty blow in the face. An enveloping dizziness came over Esther and momentarily cloaked her surroundings. She did not pass out, but everything grew dim for a considerable while.

Vaguely she was aware of being picked up and cradled against his filthy, grease-stained red-plaid woolen shirt, and then being carried by him. As she regained her senses, she continued to stay limp in his grasp, feigning unconsciousness, even though the stench of his body threatened to make her gag. Within a few minutes she heard a horse snort and realized that he had carried her back to the glen.

Esther thought Burton would set her down then, at which point she planned to leap up, sprint as best she could to Pirouette, throw herself in the saddle, and gallop away. Instead, however, he started slapping her face stingingly to bring her around while she was still in his grasp. Instinctively, she brought her hands up to her face to ward off the blows.

"Stop. Stop it!"

"Hah, so you *are* awake, eh? I thought so. You're a sneaky one. But no more of your tricks. I don't—look at me!" She had started turning her face away from him, but he grabbed her lower jaw and turned her head back so she had to look at him directly. "Look in my eyes," he said, his voice low and menacing, "so you'll know I'm speaking the truth. I don't want to kill you, but I won't hesitate to do it if you make it necessary. It's all up to you."

She knew it was no idle threat, and she was too

afraid to make a reply. After a moment he lifted her and set her astride the saddle on Pirouette. From one of the big pouches on his horse, close to the large hunting rifle in a leather saddle scabbard, he withdrew coils of rawhide tugs and said nothing more to her as he tied her in the ingenious manner in which she was now bound as she rode along on her plodding horse behind him.

Twice as they rode along this way she tried to get him to talk, to tell her where he was taking her and why. The first time he simply growled at her to shut up; the second time he stopped, dismounted, and walked back to her in so threatening a manner that she was convinced he was going to hit her again. He didn't, but he jerked so hard on the rawhide cord around her neck that she thought she would choke. He pulled a dirty, sweat-stained calico headband out of his pocket, balled it up in his grasp, and held it in front of her face.

"Iffen you don't shut up till we get where we're going," he promised her darkly, "this gets shoved into your mouth. Understand?"

She nodded, afraid even to say yes, for fear he would use it as an excuse to do just what he said. He stared full into her face for a moment and then grinned, his surprisingly even white teeth starkly framed by the black of his dense beard. Then he turned and re-mounted his horse and continued following the trail without a backward glance.

Now, having ridden at an easy gait throughout the day, he stopped when the sun was still an hour away from setting. The place he selected was a nicely sheltered, room-size clearing in an unusual triangular outcropping of rocks. At the base of the largest of the rocks, a ring of stones encircled some old ashes, and soot stains smudged the rock face—some relatively new, some very old and embedded in the grain of the rock. There was a distinct sense of great antiquity about the place, and Burton seemed familiar with his surroundings here. He untied Esther, except for the tugs that bound her wrists, and lifted her to the ground. She stood unsteadily, favoring her injured foot, surprised she could put any weight on it at all.

She decided to take the gamble that since they were no longer riding, it was safe for her to speak. "I'm thirsty," she said, surprised at the croakiness of her own voice.

"Gather up some wood for a fire," he told her, "and you'll get some water. Not until."

"But my foot hurts."

"So does my face where you gouged it. Do it!"

She turned away, already planning to flee as soon as

she got out of sight, but his next words dashed that idea.

"Don't you even *think* of tryin' to run off, woman. Like you say, your foot hurts an' your wrists are tied an' it's a long spell yet till dark. That's why we stopped early. You try to git away, I'll follow. I'll have plenty of daylight left to do it in, an' I'm a expert tracker. Iffen I have to track you down, it'll make me mad, an' onct I git mad, I do bad things to them what made me mad in the first place. So remember, if I gotta go after you, I promise you, I'll be comin' back here alone."

She believed the implicit threat, and so, limping badly and stifling the moans of pain that threatened to escape her, she made several trips to gather up twigs and limbs until he finally said there was enough. He told her to sit with her back against the rocks and, when she obeyed, he handed her a canteen of water.

Ignoring her then, Burton quickly ignited some tinder with flint and steel and built a medium-size fire inside the ring of rocks a couple of yards away from her. From another pouch he extracted the stiff carcass of a large snowshoe hare he had apparently killed and gutted sometime before encountering her. He ripped the skin from it, then used his big sheath knife to cut off the head and lower legs. He then cut the remainder in half and spitted the pieces on two pliant greenwood limbs sharpened on both ends. Shoving one end of each deeply into the ground, he angled the spits over the fire just high enough to cook the dangling meat but not to burn the wood. As soon as the meat began to sizzle and exude some of its juices, he opened a small packet and sprinkled salt lightly over both pieces.

Watching him, Esther had to admit to herself that, beast though he might be, he was also a skilled woodsman, doing what needed to be done quickly, efficiently, and with an economy of movement. As he continued to work, she looked about her. Some of the rocks in this little natural amphitheater had been marked with crude hieroglyphics — pictographs painted by the Metis, she assumed, or their forebears. But there were also others, much older, that were scratched into the rock rather than just drawn on its surface. These were symbols and lines, even words, of a character she had never before seen, somehow forbidding, and she wondered who had put them here and why. And also when.

"Eat," Burton commanded, handing her one of the spits. The meat was slightly blackened here and there but mostly roasted to a rich red-brown. It smelled good, and Esther suddenly realized that she was famished, not having eaten anything today except the dawn breakfast back at Hawk's Hill and the handful of saturated cornmeal after crossing the river. Careful not to burn herself, she tilted the spit toward her mouth and gingerly nibbled some of the meat. It was delicious.

They ate their portions in silence, Burton eating noisily, belching grossly now and again, and finishing his well before Esther finished hers. The throbbing in her leg had eased somewhat, and evidently the walking she had done to gather wood had been helpful to her rather than harmful. The foot still hurt, but apparently the puncture was not as serious as she had at first imagined.

"Why are you doing this, Mr. Burton?" she said abruptly. "Where is my son? What have you done with Ben? If you've harmed him in any way — in *any* way! — I promise you, my husband will track you down like the mad dog you are."

Burton looked at her silently, malevolently, for a long time, and when at last he spoke, his words were harsh, his voice cold.

"I see that husban' of your'n agin, first thing I do, I put a buffalo slug right through his head. You're lucky I ain't done that already to you. Would've, 'cept right now I figger you're worth more to me alive than dead."

Esther had no clear idea what he meant by that, and the dull fear within her now rose to new heights.

When she spoke, she was appalled at the near-hysteria in her own voice. "Why are you doing this to us?"

"Why? *Why!* Gawd a'mighty, woman, you dam' MacDonalds ain't caused me nothin' but trouble. Your man threatened t'kill me, you're older boy attacked me an' you yourself pointed a gun at me an' threatened t'shoot me. An' that littlest kid of your'n, I got me the notion he kilt my good ol' dawg, Lobo. Now, if that ain't—"

"You deserved all that!" she interrupted. "All that and more, for what you did. If you think—"

"Shut your mouth, woman!" he bellowed, the words striking almost with the force of physical blows. "You talk one more time 'fore I'm finished an' I'll clout you right into next Tuesday!"

Esther clamped her lips shut, knowing full well he meant it. Burton stared at her a moment longer and then resumed talking.

"Like I was tryin' t'say when you butted in, if what you MacDonalds did t'me ain't reason 'nuff fer me t'hold some bad feelin' fer your whole bunch, I don't know what is. Anyone does anything t'pain George Burton in any way—*any* way, by God!—it ain't gonna be forgot, an' sooner or later they're gonna pay fer it. An' pay-time started when I run into you. An' it's only jus' started."

He lapsed into silence then, except for noisily sucking at a tooth. At length, Esther decided to chance speaking again. She had paled at his words and her mouth had gone dry. Her own words emerged raspy and strained, in hardly more than a whisper.

"I ask you again, what have you done with my son? *Where . . . is . . . Ben?* I swear to you, if you've hurt him, I won't wait for my husband to find you. I'll do it myself. And when I do, I'll kill you for the monster you are!"

She thought he would react viciously to her words, perhaps even strike her again, but his unpredictable nature proved her wrong. He threw back his head with a loud laugh that ended in another disgusting belch, prolonged and bubbling. "You got spunk, lady." He chuckled. "I'll give you that. As for your boy, I don't know nothin' about 'im. I seed your older boy an' them two little girls of yourn in a buggy 'bout a week ago, but I ain't seen nothin' of the little runt."

Though she inwardly bristled at his referring to Ben as a runt, oddly enough, Esther thought he was telling the truth, perhaps because of her conviction that Ben was with the Metis. And because he hadn't become infuriated at her remark, she now pressed on with more questions.

"I don't understand all this. Why have you tied me up this way, and where are you taking me?"

"Wal now, I'll tell you, lady. Revenge is sweet but it don't put no money in my pocket, an' money's even better. They's three things the Injins'll pay good for—guns, redeye, an' slaves. Some of 'em, anyways. I've sold some women an chil'en to 'em afore—not t' the Metis, mebbe, but others. They gener'ly like squaws an' young'uns from other tribes, but they ain't opposed t'whites, neither. Now, since I was headin' for the Metis anyways, figgered I'll give 'em a chance t'buy you tomorrow. They pay good furs for likker an' guns, so mebbe they'll do the same for a good slave. An' iffen them Half-Breeds ain't int'rested, wal, I know some Dakotas who will be."

"You're going to *sell* me?" she gasped. "As a *slave?* Are you crazy? You can't get away with something like that. It's—it's illegal!"

"Hah! Illegal? Wal, I'll tell you somethin', lady, so's sellin' 'em firewater an' guns, but they's plenty of us what does. An' slaves, too. Jus' that slaves're a whole lot more trouble to haul aroun'. So they gotta pay good iffen they want 'em. But if these here Cree Half-Breeds don't want you when we see 'em in the mornin' an' I wind up havin' t'haul you all the way to them Dakotas, you're gonna serve me good 'long the way. Yessir, you're gonna scout up firewood like t'day an' you're gonna cook an' carry and do whatever I got in mind for you t'do. An'," he added, grinning meaningfully, "I

157

got some mighty int'restin' *other* things in mind, too, 'fore we get there."

Now the full enormity of her own terrible predicament descended on Esther MacDonald, and she began trembling uncontrollably.

CHAPTER 10

When Ben and Little Buffalo arrived at
Louis Riel's house in the morning of this eighth day
since Ben fled from Burton, they were met with some
disturbing news. Hunting Eagle had returned alone to
Singush during the night. He had reported to Riel that
upon reaching Hawk's Hill, they had approached the
house under the flag of truce, but found no one was
there. Since Otter could speak a little English, and
Hunting Eagle could not, the former elected to wait for
the MacDonalds' return, or until Hunting Eagle came
back with new instructions from Riel.

It was not only a disappointment for Ben but upset-
ting as well, and his fears soared again. Riel fathomed

what he was thinking and placed a hand on the little white boy's shoulder.

"I suspect," he said gently, "there is nothing to worry about. You are missing from your family and they are undoubtedly out looking for you. I wrote a message to them that I sent back with Hunting Eagle. He will leave it for them when he fetches Otter back here. In the meanwhile, this does not change the fact that I will be taking you back to Hawk's Hill first thing tomorrow morning."

The words did help alleviate Ben's fears somewhat, but, as their conversation went into different avenues, it was a while before he was able to focus his full attention on what they were discussing. This finally came about when the topic became the difference in the way Riel's people regarded wild creatures and the way white men did—most particularly men like George Burton.

"We Metis," Riel was saying, "are primarily hunters. We do grow a few minor crops to serve our needs, but hunting—and fishing to a lesser degree—makes up the very foundation of our existence. Yet we do not abuse nature. We do not, as too many of *your* people do, Ben, waste or destroy living creatures for sport or just to prove to ourselves that we hold the power of life or death.

"To us," he continued, "the things of nature have been provided by a higher being. To some of us, that higher being is God and to others it is Kisemanitou, the Great Spirit, who provides the animals that sustain us with their meat and give us warmth and clothing with their skins. But we do not take this for granted, and we do not take more of what nature provides than we need.

"For those deer or elk or buffalo that we kill on our hunts," he continued, "we always offer up prayers of thankfulness. You have walked about in our villages and you have seen what we do with those animals we must kill to sustain us. We do not ever kill them just for a single part, as some people kill them just for the skin, or for the best pieces of meat or, sometimes, as in the case of the buffalo, just for the *miteyaniy* and leave all the rest to go to waste."

"*Miteyaniy?*" Ben asked, remembering the word, trying to remember the meaning. And then he recalled Little Buffalo saying it as he touched his extended tongue. "*Miteyaniy?* Tongue? Some people would kill a great big buffalo just for its tongue?"

"Yes," Riel said sadly. "I once stood on a small hill in the prairie and saw before me the rotting carcasses of over three hundred buffalo from which the only thing taken by the men who killed them was their tongues."

He was quiet for a moment, seeing in his memory the grisly picture that he would never forget. When he resumed speaking, his voice was low, sorrowful.

"If we are to survive, we must hunt, but we must also do this with forethought and wisdom, for it is the way of nature to provide for our needs, but not for wastefulness. Thus, when we Metis kill an animal, we use it all—the meat, the hide, the bones, the organs, everything. And when we have taken a few animals in one place, we do not hunt there again for a long time but instead move on to another place, so the animals we have left in the first place will have the opportunity to restore their numbers in peace. Nor do we destroy the prairies and streams and forests that are the homes of these animals, because to destroy them is just another way to destroy the animals who rely on them to exist."

He smiled at Ben. "There are many animals that we greatly admire and that we feel are deserving of special respect, but these are often the types of animals that other people fear and call vermin and go out of their way to deliberately destroy—wolves and coyotes and foxes, badgers and wolverines, cougars and lynx and bobcats. And then there is the bear. Because we believe that the Great Spirit sometimes appears in the form of a bear, we never kill one unless it is absolutely necessary, as when such an animal becomes enraged and attacks and we must kill it to save our lives, or when we are threatened with starvation and no other animal is there to provide us with meat. Always, it is only with the greatest of reluctance that this is done, and we offer up prayers of apology for such an act and beg forgiveness, even though it was necessary for us to do so."

The conversation continued, touching on many aspects of Metis life, and then Riel abruptly caught himself. "The people of these villages are eager to see more of you, Ben, since they feel—as I do—that you are very special. Yet, as much as they want to see you, I have been taking most of your time. The reason is that I have enjoyed your company and our time together is running short. Tomorrow I take you back to Hawk's Hill. If your parents are still not there, I will take you to Lower Fort Garry and"—he chuckled and shook his head—"if they don't shoot me on sight, leave you in the protection of the soldiers there.

"Now, while there is still time for a little more talk, what else would you like to know?"

Ben's brow furrowed with thought and then he nodded. "There is one thing I've been wondering about. You mentioned your people being here when the Vikings came a thousand years ago. I was wondering how long the Metis or the Cree people have lived here even before that time and where they came from before that."

"As far as I know," the leader replied, "the Crees have *always* lived on these lands. That is what our traditions teach us, as far back as they are remembered. The Crees were ancient on this land when white men first came here. I don't mean the English, who first came here in 1612, but even long before that, when the great rowing ships of the Norsemen came. But they left, after a time, and then it was peaceful for a long while. Before and after that, we shared these lands only with the Assiniboine people to the west of us and the Sioux—Dakotas and Mandans—to the south. Beyond them were other tribes, but we had little contact with them except on our faraway hunts."

He paused and picked up a pine cone from a bowl on the table, then tossed it into the fire, where it began to crackle and snap. "The French came then, and they were trappers and traders. We liked them. They brought us things we had never had before and which, once we had them, we felt we could not be without, and we traded the skins of our fur animals for more. We still used the meat and other parts of these animals, but for the first time we were killing more than we could use and some of our wise men knew this was a bad thing and told these white men it was not good and they must either live as we lived or go away. Many chose to remain among us, and many of those married women of our tribe who admired them and that was the start of the Metis people."

His voice became hard and bitter as he continued. "And then the English came and they wanted furs, too. Even more than that, they wanted land. *Our* land. They stayed to themselves and considered us to be low creatures, hardly removed from the animals for whom they had no regard whatever, except for their furs. It was the true beginning of our troubles with the white man—troubles that are still with us today and that many of our people believe will continue forever, until we are all gone and the few voices that continue to protest are forever stilled. A wise man among our people, who can see things that are yet to be, has told me that my voice is one of those that will be stilled, that my days will finish at the end of an English rope. But before that happens, he said, I will light a torch that will continue to be a beacon for others to follow when I am gone. What better legacy"—he smiled—"can one leave behind than that?"

He lapsed into silence and seemed to be lost within himself for a considerable while. Ben felt some of the man's sadness in his own heart, and he wished he had the power to help Riel and his people, that he could turn the clock back to that beautiful, peaceful time that must have once been but was no more and could never be again.

Minutes passed, and at last Little Buffalo stirred, appearing as if he wished to say something. A spark of animation returned to Riel's eyes, and he beckoned the youth to speak. He did so, making a suggestion that pleased Riel and that the leader interpreted for Ben.

"This one," Little Buffalo said, touching Ben's shoulder, "has become my friend, and I think of him now as my little brother. My parents feel toward him the same warmth that I do, and we are agreed that we would like to make him a member of our family. My father has even suggested a name by which he would be known to us. We would like to call him Ka Kakekinit, not only because he has become to us a son and brother, but because it is evident that our people now believe that he is considered by the Great Spirit to be a very special person."

Riel heartily approved the idea. He placed his hands on the little boy's shoulders and with great seriousness, made it official. "Among us, hereafter, Ben, you will be known by the name of Ka Kakekinit."

Ben was very pleased and proud of such an honor and thanked them both, then added, "But I don't know what Ka Kakekinit means."

Louis Riel smiled. "Literally, it means One Found to Be the Best," he said, "But in the sense Apistchi-Paskwawi-Mustus says it, Ka Kakekinit means the Chosen One."

Unexpectedly one of the Metis men pushed past the heavy buffalo skin covering the doorway and spoke to the leader excitedly. When he finished, Riel said something to Little Buffalo, then they both came to their feet and headed for the doorway. Riel turned there and said to Ben, "Two white people on horses are just entering the village. Wait here. Little Buffalo and I will return before long."

The door flap fell into place behind them, and Ben was alone in the room. However, when a murmur of voices came to him from outside, he was unable to curb his curiosity. He peeked past the door flap and saw that a number of the villagers had gathered, in the center of whom, some forty feet away from him, now stood Louis Riel and Gabriel Dumont, with Little Buffalo standing just behind them. The growing crowd was parting somewhat to allow two riders, one behind the other, to approach their leaders.

Ben sucked in his breath with an audible fearful gasp when he recognized the first rider as indeed being the huge, bearded trapper, George Burton. On the heels of this he was flooded with a momentary exultation when he recognized the second rider as his mother. His joy was quickly dispelled, however, when he saw that her face was badly bruised, her blouse torn, her feet bare. A rage such as he had never before experienced swirled inside when he saw that she was tied to the horse like an animal.

The rage was short lived, replaced by an overwhelming determination to help his mother, a determination even stronger than his intense fear of Burton. He turned and snatched one of Riel's knives off the wall where it hung, then darted outside. Although the crowd had grown even larger, it was easy for someone as small as he to squeeze past the legs of the onlookers toward where the two horses had now come to a stop.

Unseen by either Burton or his mother, who was staring straight ahead in a dejected, fearful manner, Ben slipped through the final forest of legs and scooted under the belly of Pirouette. Then he reached up and began sawing with Riel's knife at the tugs that bound his mother's feet together. The nearby Metis saw what he was doing, and while they did not try to help him, neither did they make any move to hinder him.

Burton had nodded pleasantly enough when he stopped some ten feet in front of Riel and addressed his remarks to him, studiously avoiding eye contact with Dumont, whose steely gaze made him decidedly nervous. "I c'n talk some Cree an' some French but don't do no real good in neither one. You understand English?" When Riel inclined his head slightly in affirmation, Burton grinned. "Good. Now, then, seems I recollect meeting you afore. Mebbe two, three years ago. You're Louis Riel. You know me," he added. "I'm George Burton and I been tradin' with the Crees and other tribes for lots a'years.

"Now, I come to you peacefully," he continued blandly, "an' ever'one knows I always treat the tribes real fair in trade. What I come here for is to find out what your needs are for guns and ammunition, so I can get them for you and bring them here. In the meantime I got you something mighty nice. This," he said, turning in his saddle and indicating Esther MacDonald, "is a fine strong woman who can do lots a'hard work."

Beneath Pirouette, Ben saw Burton start to turn, and he froze in place. Fortunately, Burton was concentrating on his captive and Riel and so did not see him. Gabriel Dumont, however, had only a moment before seen Ben cutting at the tugs, and now a smile quirked the corners of his lips. He leaned over and whispered briefly to Riel, who nodded and also smiled briefly, though that expression vanished as Burton turned back to him.

"As you can see," the trapper continued, "she's healthy as a heifer and young enough to give you many years of service in whatever you got in mind for her t'do. Reckon I'd trade her to you in exchange for furs, but you got to come up with a mighty good deal 'fore I'll let 'er go."

Riel quickly raised a hand to check anything further the burly man might be ready to say. He had quite reasonably deduced—not only from Ben's actions but also from his resemblance to her—the identity of this woman behind Burton. "The Metis," he said coldly, "do not own or deal in slaves." His glance flicked for an instant to Ben, who was again sawing at the tugs, but then he looked back at Burton again with no change of expression. He then added, in the same cold tone, "It is not the way of our people to meddle in the affairs of white people when it is a matter that does not affect us personally."

Esther MacDonald had become aware that something was going on beneath her horse but at first she was not quite sure what. Then she felt one of her legs gently patted for an instant to prevent her from being startled. After a moment more, she could tell from the movement of the tugs between her ankles that someone was trying to sever the rope binding them.

"You have come into our territory and to this village

uninvited and unwanted," Riel went on, his voice now taking a decidedly menacing tone. "Since you say you have come in peace, you may leave in peace. Now."

Ben had just managed to sever the ankle tugs, and now he sprang out from under Pirouette's belly. Unable to reach high enough to cut her wrist bonds, he held a finger briefly to his lips to silence any sound she might make and then caught the mare's bridle and began cutting the long tug attached to his mother's throat.

Esther's eyes widened with unspeakable joy and relief when she saw her son, but she controlled her emotions and remained sitting still. With as strong a cut as he could manage, Ben sent the blade through the cord, and Esther quickly swung one leg over the mare's back and dropped to the ground beside her son. She had momentarily forgotten about the injured foot and uttered an involuntary gasp of pain when she landed.

Instantly Burton swiveled around in his saddle, and an ugly curse burst from his lips as he started to dismount. Esther looped her bound wrists over Ben and drew him in closely, her arms covering his chest protectively.

"Stop!"

The sharp command from Riel cut the air like a rifle shot, and Burton froze in place, half dismounted, only too aware that Dumont's rifle had almost magically appeared in his hands and the muzzle was aimed rock-steady at the center of his chest.

"Get back on your horse, Burton." Riel's order and demeanor left no room for argument.

Carefully, keeping his hands well away from his scabbarded rifle, the big trapper slid back into the saddle, his expression one of barely contained fury. He opened his mouth to speak, but a vicious chopping motion of Riel's hand quelled whatever remark he might have made.

"I told you that the Metis do not meddle in the affairs of whites unless they affect us. *This* affects us. This woman is the mother of the boy and the boy is an honored guest among us, and, as such, neither he nor his mother are to be insulted nor harmed. Turn now and leave this place while you still may. Alone! Any delay may well diminish your chances of doing so."

"You'll pay for this, Riel," Burton blustered, anger and fear waging a battle for dominance within him. Fear won. Without another word he yanked the reins, spun his horse about, and sent it into a gallop through the parting crowd the way he had come.

Even as Burton thundered off, Esther and Ben were

thanking Riel and Dumont and the gathered Metis for their help. Ben carefully cut away the tugs still binding his mother's wrists, and they hugged fiercely as soon as her arms were free. The tears she had not let herself shed before came in volume, and Ben, too, was crying with joy at their reunion. The Metis around them laughed and smiled and some came forward and gravely shook Esther's hand or gently patted her back or arm.

At a signal from Riel, the onlookers began to disperse, Dumont among them, who had matters to attend to elsewhere. In moments they were all but by themselves and Esther stepped up to Riel and took his hand in hers to shake it but then could not hold in the gratitude that engulfed her. Impulsively she leaned forward and kissed him on the cheek.

"Thank you, sir," she repeated. "I cannot express to you strongly enough how grateful we are, Ben and I. God bless you. Oh, God bless you, sir."

Some three hundred yards away from them, George Burton rode his horse past some dense bushes and small trees. The instant he was screened from view of the village, he brought the big animal to a quick stop and dismounted. The trapper tied the reins loosely to a sapling for a fast release and hasty departure, then pulled his big buffalo rifle from its scabbard and ran in a crouch back a hundred feet or more to a point where he could see the village clearly but still remain hidden.

Even from this considerable distance he could see the woman, the child, and Riel still standing about as he left them, the other Metis now having dispersed and begun moving about on their own business. The woman took Riel's hand for an instant and then kissed him on the cheek. Then she stepped back and they continued talking. Burton grinned without humor. It would be a long shot, but he was certain he could send the first bullet exactly where he wished it to go—into the woman who had once again defied him—and, with luck, the second and third shots would find their targets as well—in the runt boy who was the root of all these problems, and in that Half-Breed Riel, who had humiliated him in front of everyone. His confidence in his own ability to make such long shots was justified; many times in the past, on hunts in Saskatchewan and the Dakota Territory, he had regularly brought down buffalo after buffalo at ranges approaching twice this distance. An expert shot, he rarely missed and almost never merely wounded an animal.

Not more than fifty yards behind him, William and John MacDonald—the former mounted and the latter afoot—continued moving, as they had been since dawn. They had been chagrined when, just after sunrise, they discovered the triangular rock area where Burton and Esther had spent the night. Had father and son continued following the trail only another half-hour last evening, they would have encountered the trapper and his captive.

Now, as they moved around a bend in this trail, they jolted to a stop when they saw the tied horse. The large packs on the animal immediately identified it as Burton's. William dismounted and tied the reins to a low branch; then they held a whispered conference. In a moment they moved apart, the elder MacDonald with John's rifle about two dozen feet off on the right side of the trail and John, unarmed, close to the same distance off the trail on the left. When both were in position, they began, at a hand signal from William, to move stealthily forward, keeping alert. The brushy cover here was thick enough that they were visible to each other only at intervals.

It was John who spotted Burton first, some thirty feet ahead and taking aim, the barrel of his rifle braced in the fork of a sapling. With widening eyes, John followed the line of aim and saw three people standing close together in the open center circle of the village— a man and woman talking and a small boy next to them. Though he could not see their features, he had

175

no doubt that the woman and boy were his mother and brother.

John glanced to the right but could not see his father to signal him, and there was no time to waste. Fearing that if he made any sound to alert his father, Burton would hear it, too, the youth glanced about him and spied a smooth stone, no larger than a pine cone. He snatched it up and threw it as hard as he could, aiming at the back of Burton's head. The rock missed that mark, but struck Burton with a heavy, painful thump in the center of his broad back at the very instant the trapper squeezed the trigger.

The report of the heavy rifle was loud, and the thumb-size slug, now just slightly misdirected from Esther, kicked up a fountain of dirt within two inches of Riel's feet. Burton, cursing, whirled around and, seeing John, began swinging his rifle to bear on him. Before he could do so, however, William stepped into view some twenty feet from him, with the rifle pointed right between the trapper's eyes.

"Drop it, Burton. Drop it or you're dead. *Right now!*"

The big man let the rifle fall from his grasp, and it had hardly come to rest before John dashed in, snatched it up, and aimed it from the hip at him.

"Listen . . . listen!" Burton whined, fearful that if MacDonald didn't kill him right this moment, he would when he saw his wife's bruises. "Let me go. Keep the gun and jus' let me go. I'll git on my horse an' ride out an' you'll never see me agin." He was sniveling now. "Never. I swear it."

"Your promises aren't worth a whistle in the wind," William said. "Get your hands up—*high!* Now start walking up that trail." He motioned toward the village with the rifle barrel.

"You all right, Papa?" John asked. "If so, I'll go get the horses."

William nodded and then nudged Burton with the gun to walk faster. As they moved out of the brushy cover and into full view, they saw Riel and Dumont running toward them, leading a pack of warriors. Burton's knees nearly buckled, and now he blubbered in earnest, the words he tried to speak incoherent through his sobbing.

The Metis reached them about the same time as John, who was leading his own horse and Burton's. Two of Dumont's warriors grabbed Burton by the arms and held him, viewing the weeping man with scorn and disgust. Others from the village were coming toward them at a run, Ben and his limping mother included. And Little Buffalo beside them.

William handed the rifle to John and broke from the group, running to meet them. He swept Esther up in a great whirling embrace and then, still holding her in one arm, scooped up Ben as well, who hugged his father around the neck and kissed his grizzled cheeks. Fires of murderous rage sprang to life in William's eyes when he saw Esther's bruised cheek and arm. His fury was tempered only by Esther's insistence that she was all right, no permanent damage done.

"We have to let Mr. Riel and his people take care of whatever punishment is to be meted out to Mr. Burton," she said. "It'll probably be worse than anything we'd do. Besides, we'd get no satisfaction out of it, William, if we tried to take vengeance ourselves. We have our reward. We're together again, you and I and John and Ben, and that's what counts. And soon we'll be with the girls."

As they walked to join the group gathered around the Metis leaders and Burton, Ben swiftly related highlights of his experiences to them—the hazardous trip downriver, being rescued by Little Buffalo, and the kindness and care with which he had been treated among these generous people. By then they had reached the group, where Esther and Ben shared a joyously tearful reunion with John.

William noted that Riel and Dumont were looking on and nodding approvingly. He stepped over to them and, in turn, shook their hands.

"Thank you," he said. "Thank you for saving my son and caring for him. For saving my wife from him." He jerked his thumb in the direction of Burton, now sitting with his head resting on his knees, face hidden. "I don't think I can ever fully repay you for what you have done."

When Riel interpreted for Dumont, the war leader spoke in French briefly and Riel put his words into English. "What my good friend Gabriel says is from his heart, and his words are mine as well. He says, 'Tell these white people that we may be of different races, but we are all human outside and brothers inside; that it is the wish of the Great Spirit that we think little of how we differ, and greatly of how we are alike and need one another.' It is true. There has to be—there *is*—a brotherhood among us all, and we must never forget that." He smiled shyly. "That is something I was taught when I studied for the priesthood," he said, "but it didn't mean quite so much then as it does at this moment."

Riel touched William's arm and spoke in a brisker tone. "Come, bring the others with you and let's sit and talk together awhile. I would like to hear from you and your wife about how each of you came to arrive here in different ways. As for *him*"—he tilted his head toward Burton—"let him simmer in his fears over what is in store for him. The dread of what is to befall preys heavily upon the mind and most often is much worse than the actuality."

The seven of them—Riel, Dumont, William, Esther, John, Ben, and Little Buffalo—moved apart and sat down in a circle, shaded by the only tree nearby. For upward of an hour they talked together, each speaking of his part in this incident. At last they rose and returned to where the warriors were ringed about Burton.

Riel stepped over to where some of the warriors had set Burton's two large packs on the ground and were inspecting the contents, some of which had been piled to one side. Among the goods were half a dozen pairs of new, well-made, and elaborately decorated elkskin moccasins, evidently secured by Burton during his trading stint at Oiseau. The Metis leader selected a pair and brought them back to Esther.

"These may not be an exact fit," he said, smiling, "but they'll be close, and they'll certainly protect your feet."

As Esther thanked him and sat down on the ground to put them on, Riel turned and issued a command to a pair of muscular young warriors nearby. The two nodded and began replacing the stacked items inside the two packs. As they did so, Riel spoke further to them in Cree. The warriors acknowledged their leader's instructions with grins and a few words in response, and then, each carrying one of the heavy bags, set off for the village. Riel's gaze moved to settle on Burton and his horse, the latter with the big buffalo gun back in its scabbard, where John had put it.

"As for this man's horse and his rifle," Riel said coldly, staring stonily at the trembling trapper, "they are being confiscated, as his goods have been, in punishment for his attempted murders." He turned to face William, and his expression softened. "Horse and gun are now yours, to replace those you lost in crossing the river."

Nonplussed at this unexpected act of generosity, William thanked him and then stepped to Burton's horse and took the big buffalo gun out of the saddle scabbard. He returned with it to Gabriel Dumont and extended it to him. "A little while ago," he said, "you told us how much it meant to you when you were fourteen and were honored by being given your first gun, which you still have after all these years. Perhaps it would give you pleasure to honor some other young man with his first gun." He tilted his head toward Little Buffalo, who, off to one side, was engaged in a quiet conversation with one of the warriors.

Dumont, on hearing Riel's interpretation, bowed his head deeply to William in acknowledgment. Turning then, he strode to Little Buffalo and handed the gun to the youth, speaking a few words to him softly in the Cree tongue. The Metis boy, obviously nonplussed, could not reply, and though he tried, neither could he check the tears that silently dribbled from his eyes and down his cheeks.

His own eyes now a hint overbright, Louis Riel looked at the Metis boy proudly. Then he glanced northward and smiled as he saw that the two runners who had taken Burton's packs to the village were now returning on the run with another pair of packs that were similar but smaller. As they slowed, then stopped near the group, he again turned his attention to those near him and moved to where Esther was standing with one arm around Ben, the other linked in her husband's. John stood on the other side of Ben. Riel looked at the little family group gravely.

"You are good people," he said. "I owe you my life; a debt that will not be forgotten. It would honor us if you would return to the village with us now and be our guests for what food and lodging we can provide you, for as long as you wish."

"We're the ones," William replied, "who have been honored by you, and we owe you more than we have the ability to pay. We—all of us—thank you for your kind and generous offer and hope you won't be offended if we don't accept. We've been away from our home and our girls for too long. They must be extremely anxious for all of us; they already believe Ben is dead and now are undoubtedly concerned for our safety, too. We think it's important that we return to them at once, to relieve their minds and take them home, where we can all be together once again as a family."

He paused, as if finished, but then shook his head. "No. I'm not being completely honest with you, and I *must* be, if I'm to be able to live with myself after all this." He took a deep breath and seemed to steel himself before continuing. "I'm one of the far too many whites who have held you Metis people in contempt. And I'm deeply ashamed to admit that I've often spoken of the Metis disparagingly as Half-Breeds. I was willing to condemn you without even knowing you, simply because your culture and background differ from mine. I not only didn't understand you, I didn't make any *attempt* to understand you. Worse yet, I forced my own distorted views on my family and taught them to dislike — even distrust and fear — a whole race of people simply because of my own ignorance.

"I know better now, and I will not again speak harmfully about you, nor tolerate anyone in my presence who does so. Nor will I raise my hand against you under any pretext, nor count as friends any who would. That's perhaps a start in the right direction, I think, but it doesn't ease my shame for how I've felt and acted. We've received far better treatment in your hands than you would have received in ours had the situation been reversed."

He scuffed his shoe in the dirt and looked at it without seeing it. Finally he raised his head and looked at Louis Riel directly. "I am truly sorry, and I want you to know that from now on, the doors of our home at Hawk's Hill are always open in welcome to you—to all the Metis in fact—and we would feel our lives blessed and our home honored any time you might care to visit us."

When he stopped, it was Esther who spoke up. "I have to echo everything my husband has said," she told him. "Mr. Riel, our words alone simply can't express how grateful we are. Please consider our house to be your house. And whatever the future might hold, you can always count on our friendship."

The seven shook hands with genuine warmth all around. Ben and Little Buffalo stood looking at each other for a long time, both feeling a welling of emotion that defied expression in their limited ability to communicate, but what they said with their eyes and the clasping together of their hands transcended words. At last they embraced in a prolonged hug that each knew was an unspoken pledge to remain brothers in their hearts forever.

Then there was still the matter of George Burton.

As Riel approached and stopped an arm's length in front of him, the trapper, devoid of horse, goods, and gun, again began trembling uncontrollably, no doubt believing that he was now to be executed. The Metis leader viewed him with unconcealed distaste, and Ben, watching closely, somehow knew that he would never again be afraid of any man the likes of George Burton.

"You do not die today," Riel said in a deadly level voice. "Unlike you, the Metis do not harm those who are helpless in their grasp. You have three days in which to leave this valley forever. You will not be harmed during that period, but if you are seen after that, you will surely die. If you return to this valley at some later date, you will surely die; the Metis have long memories. If you should ever attempt to harm the MacDonald family in any way, here or elsewhere, you will be hunted down, no matter the distance, and be dealt with as the Metis deal with any mad dog they encounter. Go now, and do not delay. Remember, three days only. Go!"

Burton began shuffling away, gradually picking up speed until he was running as fast as he could, occasionally glancing fearfully over his shoulder. In less than a minute he disappeared into the brush.

Then it was time for the MacDonalds to leave as well. Esther's mare had been brought out to them from the village, and now all four of them mounted up; Esther on Pirouette, John on his gelding, and William with Ben in the saddle before him on the horse that had been Burton's.

Louis Riel approached, carrying over his arm the two packs that the young warriors had brought back from the village. "It was no surprise that you would be in haste to return to your daughters," he told William and Esther, looking from one to the other. "It would have been a great surprise to us had you not been. It was why I had our young men bring me these pouches." He looped them over Pirouette's back directly behind Esther's saddle. "You have a long ride ahead of you to reach your home. Inside these"—he tapped a pouch and then stepped back—"you will find enough good food that you may eat well during your journey. There are flasks of water, as well. And there are a few minor gifts that it pleases us to give you—mementos you may wish to keep to remind you of this time that brought us together in fear and saw us separate in friendship."

He moved to William's horse and smiled up at Ben. "It has been an important occasion for the Metis to have had you among us. We believe that there are strange and wonderful things in store for you, that what we and others have seen is but a small part of what will eventually come to be. For now, we wish you a safe journey home. And," he added, reaching up and gently squeezing one small hand, "never forget that while to your family and to others you are Ben MacDonald, to us you are also, and always will be Ka Kakekinit—the Chosen One."

Beth and Coral MacDonald sat quietly on the swing seat hanging from chains on the sprawling veranda of the MacComber farm, the best place from which they could see the approach of anyone from either direction. The MacCombers were characteristically busy with their own affairs—Mary in the kitchen beginning to trim and cut long, crisp stems of rhubarb for the pie she was going to bake, Dan in the barn mending harnesses that had become frayed.

Both girls were convinced that Ben was dead, and the awful emptiness this left within them was a gap that they were certain could never be filled. Previously he had simply been their little brother, cute in some ways, irksome in others, more often tolerated than appreciated. Each remembered how often it occurred that, with no other boy even near his age anywhere for miles around, Ben would go off by himself and walk alone or sit beneath a tree for long periods, a tiny monument to loneliness. Each knew in her heart that she could have eased that loneliness by going to him, talking with him, *listening* to him. Instead, they mostly ignored him and concentrated more on their own bickering with each other. That bickering had ended with Ben's disappearance, and both girls were certain it wouldn't occur again, but that didn't ease the emptiness.

Abruptly tears filled Coral's eyes and began trickling down her cheeks. Beth noticed, moved closer, and put her arm around her little sister comfortingly. "What?" she asked.

Coral sobbed aloud now, and her words were broken. "I . . . I don't remember ever . . . ever telling him, Beth."

"Telling who what?"

"Ben. I don't remember ever telling him that I loved him. I'd give anything if I could have the chance again. Now I never will."

Beth nodded, and her own voice was unsteady when

she responded. "I know, Coral. Me, too. Why couldn't we have been a little kinder? It wouldn't have been so hard, would it?"

Coral shook her head but didn't reply, and they were silent again for a long while. From inside the house they could hear dishes rattling, and in the sheep pen a lamb bleated plaintively.

"I'm scared, Coral," Beth said.

The younger girl nodded, knowing at once what she meant. "Me, too. I've been too scared to even talk about it. You think they'll ever come back?"

"I don't know, Coral. I don't know what we'd do if they didn't. It's been bad enough about Ben, but if— if—" She couldn't go on.

"Girls, that's enough!" It was Mary MacComber, standing in the doorway, her bib apron dusted with flour, her voice edged with sternness. "You're thinking too much about what *might* be and not enough about what *is*. Folks do that, they get a lot more heartache than need be. Clouds the mind."

"But they might be dead!" Coral sobbed. "Mama and Papa and John. They might never come back."

"And they might, too," Mrs. MacComber said, her voice becoming more gentle. "*That's* what you have to believe, what you have to have faith in. You get your eyes all filled with tears, you can't see what's on the horizon." She paused and then disappeared back inside the house.

The sisters sat still, silent now; there seemed to be nothing left to say. After a long while Coral raised her head listlessly, but then suddenly stiffened and gasped. Beth heard her and looked in the same direction, and then she abruptly squealed. Three riders were coming their way in the long MacComber lane. Mama. Papa. John. And in the saddle in front of Papa, a much smaller figure.

Ben.

Skirt held high off the ground, Beth was off the veranda in an instant and racing down the lane to meet them; Coral, short legs pumping furiously to keep up, was not far behind. As the girls and riders neared one another, the horses stopped and the riders dismounted. The six flew into each other's arms, and there were tears and cries of joy and names repeated over and over and an abundance of hugs and kisses. When all the hubbub subsided a little, William stood with one arm over Beth's shoulders, the other hand cupping Coral's neck and holding her close.

"It's been quite a time for all of us," he said, "and too long since we've all been together like this as a family."

"Much too long," Esther agreed, one arm around John's waist, the other hand holding Ben's. "We've been blessed," she added, "and I think we should take a moment to thank God, silently, each of us in his own way."

She bowed her head, and the other five did the same. For fully a minute they stood that way, linked in their faith in God and their love for one another. It was John who voiced the "Amen" for all of them.

"Now," Esther said, lifting her head and smiling, "I think we better go up to the house and thank Mary and Dan and then head for Hawk's Hill."

"Amen to that, too," John put in. "All I want is a bath and to sleep for a week or so."

"Sounds like a grand idea to me, John," William said, grinning. "How about you, Ben? You've been away longer than any of us. Are you ready to go home?"

Ben looked at his family, and his smile reflected the glow he felt inside. "I'm with all of you again," he said. "I'm already home."